The Last Stop

First published by BlackBird Books in 2017

10 Orange Street
Sunnyside
Auckland Park 2092
South Africa
+2711 628 3200
www.jacana.co.za

ISBN 978-1-928337-43-0

Cover design by Shawn Paikin
Set in Sabon 10.5/14pt
Printed and bound by ABC Press, Cape Town
Job no. 002995

See a complete list of BlackBird Books titles
at www.jacana.co.za

The Last Stop

Thabiso Mofokeng

BLACKBIRD
BOOKS

To Mido Macia (1985–2013)

African continent, you deserve to be united – now and for a better future.

One

MACKO WOKE. IT was already light outside. He always woke very early so that he had time to arrive at the taxi rank and register his taxi for the day's trips. He noticed that Rose was still snoring. He picked up his cellphone and pressed its buttons. He stared at the screen and made his eyes small. Its light struck his retinas. He placed it aside. It was cold, and he pulled the blankets up and covered his head. He fell asleep.

Macko woke again. Abruptly, this time. A voice next to him calling: "In the name of Jesus! In the name of Jesus! In the name of Jesus!" It was Rose's voice. At first Macko thought he was dreaming. He blinked. The words continued, more insistent: "In the name of Jesus! In the name of Jesus! In the name of Jesus!"

He sat bolt upright, scared. Questions flooded his mind. Before he could ask them, there was a bang on the window of the bedroom. Macko and Rose turned their heads at the same time. They stared at the windowpane. The room was silent again. Macko felt a shudder rise up from his stomach. He stared at the corrugated-iron roof.

"I dreamt a giant thing that I couldn't really see was entering the house. It came in and stirred at the water in the bucket. As I approached it, it lifted the bucket to sprinkle me with that water, which seemed to boil," Rose said, with teary eyes.

Macko shook his head.

Rose continued, "When I started crying, it flew to the window and disappeared."

Macko pressed his hands together to stop them shaking. He didn't want Rose to know he was afraid. As he grew calmer, he pulled Rose towards him under the blankets. They lay holding each other tight. Only their breath was heard, no talk.

Macko's breathing was slow and loud. Rose looked at him, and touched his face: "Babe, wake up!"

Macko startled at the touch of her hand. He blinked with reddish eyes. "I am awake!" he answered, getting out of bed. He stood on the cold floor in his Scotch boxers and leopard-skin print vest. His machine was erect, making it obvious that he wanted a taste of Rose's pretty pink vagina.

"It is nearly eight o'clock. Don't take long at the funeral. Remember the road to Vereeniging is very long, and it's you who is taking the first load tomorrow." That was a serious Rose, ignoring Macko's big machine.

"Yes, I know. You, you like to tell me the things I already know," Macko said briskly, barely concealing the annoyance in his voice. As he was about to leave the bedroom, he saw the water in the bucket moving. Small ripples ran over the surface as if it had been stirred. His head suddenly felt cloudy, as if it was also being stirred. He knocked into the counter in the kitchen, his balance momentarily lost. He was not feeling himself at all.

"Please, don't break my things!" Rose called from the bedroom. "May you tell me, why are you supposed to attend that child's funeral?"

Macko gripped the counter and stood for a second before he answered. “That poor child was hit by a stray bullet, because of the taxi violence near Sasolburg. That bullet was meant for me, and it was me who called the police to that incident. Do you know what is damn sad about it? The poor child was just trying to pick up his mother’s oranges that had fallen and scattered. He was helping his poor mother, who was trying to put food on the table. So I should attend his funeral,” Macko said. His found his eyes were wet and mucus was running from his nose.

He wiped his face and filled the kettle. While waiting for it to boil, he headed outside, still wearing only his underwear. The morning air hit him, and he flinched at the cold. Moving quickly, he checked if his taxi was still in the same condition he’d left it in the night before. All seemed fine with his beloved scrap. The red paint shone in the thin sunlight. On the back windscreen, below the words “When days are dark friends are few”, the Orlando Pirates sticker was starting to peel.

He stretched his body under the early-morning sun’s weak rays. Getting no warmth, he returned to the kitchen. He poured the boiling water into the washing basin, then mixed in the cold water. He washed in the kitchen, where it was warmest. The sun streamed through the window, warming the kitchen first, before the other rooms. He started with his face. Then on to the stomach and the back. He washed his shaven head. Then the waist and the feet. He dried himself and got out of the basin, smeared his body with lotion. He shivered, his skin pricking like that of a chicken. He threw the water outside, then went to the bedroom, and dressed hurriedly. He made himself a soft porridge, emptied it into a bowl, and went outside. He unlocked his taxi, took his seat, and started the ignition. He drank his soft porridge. The taxi warmed up. He returned to the house, dropping the dish in the sink. In the bedroom, he found Rose sleeping. He shook his head: "This was the person telling me to wake up, look at her!"

He put on his hat, left the bedroom, pulled the front door shut and was out of the house. He started the taxi and set off. In his rearview mirror, he saw his small puppy chasing after him, barking. He hit the road, the puppy trailing him until finally it tired near the corner. He watch the puppy walk back, only to set off again after another car.

On the side of the road leading from Thababosiu, his village in Qwaqwa, passengers wanting to get to the main rank in Setsing tried to stop Macko, but he drove past them. He did not halt at the stop signs either.

"If I can at least arrive before they go to the grave," he said aloud.

After driving for over two hours, Macko arrived in time to see the funeral procession leaving the church for the cemetery. He immediately joined the line of mourners heading to the graveside. Like the other cars and taxis in the procession, he flicked on his parking lights. Finally, they arrived at the cemetery.

"With so many people, it's hard to believe it is the funeral of a child, and equally hard to believe it is during the week," Macko said to himself as he parked his taxi.

He joined the other mourners getting out of their cars. Old men took the coffin out of the hearse. There was weeping among the women. They walked slowly to the grave and gathered around it. The pastor started the service with a prayer. There was a hymn. The family was asked to pour the soil in the grave, then the other mourners were given an opportunity to do so. Men showed themselves. Women went back. Weak men also went back. Those who wore white suits and light-coloured clothing also went back.

Macko went back. He was stopped by a figure. A man. His face was in shadow, despite the sunlight. Macko blinked, trying to make out his features. For a moment he thought it might be one of the drivers from a rival taxi association, and he felt his body tense, his eyes casting around. The other mourners were half-way across the cemetery, walking in small clusters, the occasional figure alone, lost in grief. It was just Macko and the man. He had no choice. He stepped forward to get a better view of his face, saw it twist – not so much a grimace as a wavering – and then rush into focus. It was the detective investigating the boy's death. He remembered the name: Detective Baile. Macko had talked to him briefly at the scene. Now he smiled, even though he didn't particularly want to talk to the man – he had his routes to get to.

"Sir!" said the detective, offering his hand to greet Macko.

"Good morning, sir," Macko replied quietly. He reached out his hand in response, gripped the detective's outstretched hand, then pulled back, surprised by how cold it was, cold and limp, almost lifeless. "I'm sorry…" he started to say. He didn't want the man to think he was rude or unco-operative. He couldn't say what had come over him. Maybe it was tiredness, or the stress of the funeral? Detective Baile seemed unfazed. He spoke in a clear, urgent voice that seemed somehow familiar to Macko – more familiar than it should be, considering the brevity of their first meeting. He asked Macko to wait for him.

There were a few things he needed to take care of, but it was important that they spoke before Macko left. "I need to ask you some questions, as you said you saw everything," he said, grabbing hold of Macko's arm as if to stress the importance of his words. "I won't be long. Please wait for me." With that he turned and followed the path the other mourners had taken towards the car park.

Macko stood and watched him go. He blinked against the glare, lifted his hand to shield his eyes from the sun. When he looked again, the man had vanished. He tried to find him. Cast his eyes around the cemetery. Walked a few steps forward to get a better view of the parking area and looked from face to face. He watched the last of the mourners pay their respects to the parents of the dead boy, then climb into their vehicles. The detective was nowhere to be seen. Had he really seen him?

Macko stood until the last car left. Now he was alone in the cemetery except for a few lone mourners who had come to pay their respects to their dead. He paced up and down. He remembered the detective's words, the urgency in his voice. He folded his arms and rocked on his heels. Ten minutes passed, then fifteen. He was going to be late. He paced some more.

He was about to leave when he thought he heard a sound from somewhere beneath him. He stopped and looked down at the fresh sand on the grave. As he stared, it seemed to him that the grave had begun to rise, the soil falling away slowly. He rubbed his eyes. He was probably suffering from a lack of sleep. The soil was still falling, faster now.

He looked around at the scattering of mourners at distant graves. Could anyone else see what he was seeing? He tried to shout, to get their attention.

He opened his mouth, but nothing came out. He couldn't move, couldn't cry out, couldn't take air into his lungs. He was frozen for what seemed like forever. Finally he felt a hot trickle down his leg. He had pissed himself. The shock knocked him out of his stupor. He stepped back from the grave. Started to run, then tripped and fell to his knees in the dirt. Something had blocked him: two shoes. He lifted up his head to see the man's face, but the legs didn't end. All he saw were dusty shoes and then long, unending brown trousers.

He didn't wait any longer. He jumped to his feet, spun around, and started to run. He could see his taxi in the distance. He ran blindly. The scattering of other visitors in the cemetery lifted their heads as he passed. He didn't stop. He reached his taxi, throwing himself against the door. Finally safe behind the wheel, he breathed out. He was out of harm's way in his scrap. Everything was fine, familiar. He turned the key in the ignition, shifted the gear from neutral to first, and pressed the accelerator. The handbrake was down, but the taxi didn't move. It made no sense. He pressed the accelerator harder. The wheels spun and black clouds of smoke erupted from the exhaust. He now had the attention of everyone at the cemetery. At the main gate at the edge of the compound, the guard started towards him. He tried again. Again, nothing. He was about to give up, when the vehicle lurched forward. He accelerated, breathed deeply, and started the journey back to Qwaqwa.

Macko felt something moving across his scalp, but nothing was there. People flooded the pavement, waiting for a taxi. It was dense with the heat of them, clustered in large groups, but speaking in quiet voices. Among them was a middle-aged lady. Elegant, formally dressed as if for church or a funeral. Her makeup was perfect. She took a small portable mirror out of her purse and looked at herself. Those around her paid no attention. They touched her as they passed, but didn't seem to feel her or see her.

As Macko drew nearer, she stepped forward, pushed to the front of the crowd, raised her hand, hid the thumb, showing four fingers to indicate her destination. There were only three seats left. She took the last space at the back, leaving two seats behind the driver's seat. She pushed her way down the narrow passage, head slightly bent. Smoothed her skirt and sat down. The stop had interrupted the flow of the conversation. People were laughing aloud when the taxi door opened, but now they were silent. They waited for the driver to pull off again before continuing their conversations.

"I am telling you, I am very tired. That kid's funeral in the morning was very terrible for me. I think that kid is after me," said Macko.

The passengers clicked their tongues in sympathy.

The taxi stopped to drop a man at his destination, and picked up an old man. Macko waited for him to get comfortable. He kept glancing in the rearview mirror.

"Mama, where are you going?" he asked the middle-aged lady.

She didn't reply.

"Mama! Where are you going?" he said again.

As she was about to answer him, moving her lips, more passengers waved him down from the pavement. Once he had stopped, he looked into the mirror again. His eyes were directly on the lady.

"Please, your destination."

"I am going to the Post Office, my child," the old man replied.

"I am not talking to you." There was irritation in Macko's voice.

"Are you asking me, grootman? I am going to Shoprite," a passenger at the back answered.

"I am also not talking to you!" he said, looking in the mirror again. The elegant middle-aged lady had vanished. He blinked, and the taxi pitched to the left. The passengers let out a cry in unison.

"My grootman, who are you speaking with?"

The old man clapped his hands once and asked, "Did they bewitch you, child?"

Macko righted the wheel. He shifted in his seat. He set off again, faster this time, weaving through the traffic, jumping lanes, despite the protests. He dropped the final passengers at their destinations, and the taxi was empty at last. He sat awhile, hands still on the wheel. He breathed deeply.

After counting his money, he set off again, staring ahead through the windscreen. Suddenly there was someone right in front of him – the woman he had previously seen in his taxi. She stepped forward and raised her hand exactly as before, the same gesture, showing four fingers to indicate her destination, the same destination. Macko blinked. He stared at her. Something was wrong. Something was happening. It was the same woman, her face was the same, her bright eyes and tight lips, but her body was transforming. Macko was staring at a man. Shit, it was a policeman. His jaw dropped. His foot slid with it, the taxi revving forward. Macko's eyes grew wide, his mouth limp. He turned the steering wheel just in time, and the tyres skidded on the tar. He tried to hit the brakes, but the momentum thrust him forward onto the gearshift.

The taxi slid, slamming the pavement before flipping over and slamming down again, metal on tar. A loud bang, and then silence.

Slowly the door opened and Macko got out. He was sweating, dazed, but he wasn't injured, not even a scratch. He dusted himself off, turned back to his taxi, a pile of mangled metal. A crowd had started to gather. The smell of smoke and the sounds of sirens, louder and louder. The policeman vanished. A young girl pushed her way to the front. She said his name softly and looked right in his eyes: "You must go home, to the country of your forefathers. Otherwise you are going to die."

Then she vanished. Macko was alone, holding his head. He looked at the wreck of his taxi and saw it standing on all four wheels, no more damaged than usual. He blinked his eyes faster and shook his head slower.

Two

Macko was driving so slowly he was holding up the traffic behind him. There was a black jeep directly on his tail-lights. The driver was obviously in a hurry. He had already overtaken the seven-car-deep backlog that had built up behind Macko's taxi. Still Macko held his ground, refusing to make way for the jeep. The oncoming traffic was heavy, and its driver had no choice but to decrease speed. He flashed his lights, but Macko deliberately ignored the signal. He watched in the rearview mirror as the jeep swerved out of its lane before being forced back by the oncoming traffic. The driver was taking chances. The road was narrow here and filled with sharp turns and curves. Macko pulled his eyes away from the mirror and focused them back on the side of the road, scanning for passengers and hooting to attract commuters. The oncoming traffic started to thin, and behind him the jeep tried to overtake again.

The jeep driver shot his hand out his open window, shouting and showing Macko his middle finger as he sped past. He had almost passed when another taxi appeared from around a bend in the oncoming lane. Its driver, seeing the jeep, started to brake then eased off, obviously realising he was travelling too fast.

Instead, he put his foot flat down on the accelerator, hit his hooter and flicked his lights at the oncoming jeep. As the taxi sped towards them, Macko could see the faces of the commuters through the windscreen, church mothers frozen in their Sunday attire, mouths moving, probably in prayer, others with their hands on their heads, faces locked in silent screams.

"See, see those with the luxury cars. They think they are better than us, the taxi drivers," Macko said to no one. He didn't bother to decrease his speed to allow the jeep to return to its correct lane. Behind him, a mother travelling with her two children closed her eyes and clasped her children's arms as if that might somehow protect them. The children struggled free and continued with their games, unaware of any danger. At the last moment the taxi in the opposite lane decreased its speed and swerved slightly onto the shoulder of the road to give the jeep the space it needed. It flew past with only seconds to spare.

"But my brother, you are driving shit for us," said the mother, her face flushed with fear.

Macko was about to respond with insults in his mouth, but then he glanced in the mirror and saw the mother's face, the fear and hurt in her eyes, and how she held tightly onto her children. Macko began to calm down. "Please forgive me, mme." He started to explain the difficulties he faced, the numbers the owner of his taxi demanded.

"Please don't make us to suffer just because the owner of your taxi treats you badly," said the woman. "We don't have anything to do with what is between you. We are not guilty at all!" She started to cry and seeing their mother crying, the children began to cry as well. The sounds of soft sobbing filled the taxi, and Macko scratched his head.

"Eish," he nodded, seeing that the woman spoke the truth.

"Now see how the windows of this taxi are cracked. We are not safe at all!" the mother said while trying to comfort her children.

Macko was silent. He shook his head, pushing away the soft "kiri kiri kiri" sound that came from somewhere below the wheels.

Like all the other taxis on the road, Macko was riding his hooter hard, really pumping it. Passengers didn't have money for taxi fare at this time of the month. The taxis drove empty, especially on Thursdays, when most people chose to walk, regardless of the distance. They were saving what little money they had left for the essentials – things like bread, sugar, tea.

"Don't you want to ride?" Macko shouted at a young sister. The girl wore a neatly ironed jean-skirt, with a blue flowered blouse and formal shoes, a handbag on her shoulder. Her hair was short and dyed a maroon colour. Her light skin matched the dye. Macko could tell from her outfit that she was going to town.

The sister shook her head.

"I know you are going to town. You can pay me only half of your fare. Only five!"

"Brother, please leave me alone!" This was a sister with rudeness. She focused her eyes forward and continued to walk along the road that led to town.

Every person has their own challenges, thought Macko. "Ag sies, I was just helping you out. I know you girls. By the time that you arrive in town, you will have dirt on your feet. There's no one who is going to look at you."

But the sister waved her hand and continued with her walking.

"I was just trying to help her, mother," Macko said, glancing back at the woman who was still clutching her children. She answered him with a black look and Macko sighed, then increased the volume on his CD player. Traditional gospel music blared from the speakers.

Despite the volume of the music, the whistle was still audible. It was a sharp sound that broke through the gospel melody and made Macko jump. He hit the brakes and the taxi dragged to a stop, scraping along the tar and sending up clouds of dark smoke from the front tyres. The bakkie behind him skidded to a halt. Glancing at his rearview mirror, Macko saw the occupants were an old couple. He watched the driver take off his eyeglasses and open his door. He was shouting, "Hey, you! Is it your mother who gave you driving lessons? You almost killed us."

The old woman followed him out: "Please let him go, my husband. Let us leave. God will deal with him!"

Macko stared at the old people, uncertain how to respond. He put his elbow on the open window of his taxi and leaned out. Despite the hour, everything looked very bright, and he blinked against the glare. His head had started to pound; a hollow "Kutu kutu! Kutu kutu!" like the rhythmic beats of traditional drums. He opened his eyes wide. "Kutu kutu! Kutu kutu!"

"Pull a move like that again and you will hate the day you were born!" said the old man, making a snapping gesture with his hand as if it held a sjambok. The old woman grabbed at her husband, snaring him by his trousers, and pulled him back to their vehicle. They got into their bakkie, the old man swearing all the way. Not all his words reached Macko's ears, but he could tell by their tone that they were fighting words. He noted the rusty corrugated iron in the back of the truck. Behind them, other drivers were pressing their hooters, filling the air with a din that swallowed up the old man's voice. A few taxi drivers had their hands out of their taxis, waving at the old couple.

"Fok maan! This is not your road!"

"You, old man, you are trouble. Please stop driving, you are going to kill us," shouted another driver, his head out the window of his taxi.

The old man threw up his hand at them. He started the ignition of his bakkie. The motor sputtered, then lurched and died. It took a few attempts before the engine took. Finally it started. The bakkie pulled off and turned at the corner, a trail of exhaust fumes billowing behind it. Black smoke obscured the view for a moment. By the time it evaporated, the bakkie was gone.

"Hey, my broer. An old man gave you a hard time," said Dodo, a taxi marshal at the local taxi rank, as he got into Macko's taxi.

"Hey, my broer, today is not my day. I am telling you the truth!" Macko was shaking his head.

Dodo laughed. "What is wrong, my dog?"

"I thought you were a passenger, or you are going to pay me today?" Macko looked Dodo in the eyes.

"Before your day gets worse, please leave me right here, I will take another taxi," said the mother with the children.

"Please wait, my sister. We are already at the town!" Macko said, changing gears.

The mother kept quiet.

"So, my broer, why is this taxi so bad like this? The windows are cracked. The doors are bent, and are opening hard. The lights on the right side are broken. What is going on?" Dodo asked Macko.

"You know that I don't drive local, right?"

"Yes, I am surprised! What is the problem?"

"Yesterday I took the passengers to Vereeniging. Things were really bad when I passed Sasolburg, and when I arrived in Vereeniging, it was worse. Things were very bad there. Men died, some of them drivers. And then a child was killed, shot by one of the drivers. I don't even want to remember that tragedy. It doesn't want to leave my head."

"My dog! What was going on?"

"Nxa!"Macko's eyes were wet.

"Eish, eish, sorry, my dog," Dodo said, holding his gaze, then looking down and away.

"Tabola and his friends won't reach an agreement with the Gauteng Taxi Association. Gauteng taxis come here to Free State carrying passengers, so why shouldn't they return with a load of the passengers, just like our taxis?" asked Macko.

"This issue is going to kill many people, my broer. Yes, I also ask myself why we on this side go to Gauteng loaded with passengers and return loaded with passengers, but Gauteng taxis should have to return empty. Your boss, Mr Tabola, is so stubborn and full of pride." Dodo shook his head and clapped hands. "Wait, wait, there is a passenger."

Macko turned to the pavement and saw a bald man, busy with his phone. He hit his hooter to check if the man was indeed looking for a taxi. The man glanced at Macko, then turned his head and kept walking.

"No, this man doesn't want to ride with us," said Macko, taking his hand off the hooter.

Dodo looked at the man and called, "He's coming, look."

"This person is not willing to go with us."

"He is coming, just wait and see," said Dodo.

"You know, passengers are so annoying

sometimes!" Macko said, tap-tapping his feet, raising the dust had that gathered in the footwell. The man they were waiting for opened the door and got inside. He did not greet anyone. He closed the door of the taxi, hard. Everyone heard the disturbing sound: "Qhuuuu!" as the door crashed into the dust. The passengers froze. They shut their eyes, then opened them slowly. The two children started to cry again. "Ag man!" said Dodo. He was already out of the taxi, helping the passenger with the door. They got it back on, but now the door catch was loose. "This thing does not work," exclaimed the passenger.

Dodo pressed the door, took a screwdriver from his pocket, bent some of the wires, and the door managed to catch again. He hopped into the front passenger seat and closed the door behind him.

Macko didn't say anything. "Kutu kutu! Kutu kutu!" His head was filled with the rhythmic pounding of a traditional doctor's beats again. After a few minutes, the drumming inside his skull subsided. He turned around. "My sir, what is written next to you?"

The man looked around, confused. Finally his eyes settled on a small sign pasted to the metal of the taxi's interior.

"Here?" He pointed. "It is written, 'Notice: Close the door nicely when you enter or leave this taxi. Don't slam the door. Don't be angry at the door. Please, dear passenger.'"

"When you enter the taxi, sir, your eyes should fall directly on this notice because it's right opposite the door, isn't that correct?" asked Macko.

"Yes, it's true, my good sir. It is my mistake, please forgive me," the passenger said calmly.

"And still you choose to finish off my taxi even though you can see its current condition?"

"Sir, if you want to leave this taxi, tell me in a polite manner." The passenger's anger began to mount. "There are many taxis to ride! I am not begging you at all."

Macko wanted to tell the passenger to get out. But when he looked at the money he had made that day, he hesitated. He kept quiet.

After a moment Dodo asked, "So, my dog, do you think this feud between the long-distance taxi drivers will end?"

"I don't think so. If Tabola continues not to care about other people's lives, I will soon be dead. I almost died yesterday. If you had seen that fight, you would understand what I mean. They poured petrol over my taxi, wanting to burn it while I was inside. Just think!"

The paved streets indicated that they had arrived in town. Macko checked the time on his phone. It was twenty-four minutes past eleven. It was time to make money for those who knew how. White men wearing suits and ties carrying their briefcases were heading towards the bank. Six comrades wearing their EFF T-shirts and berets were coming from the municipal offices.

Macko drove without paying much attention to his surroundings. He glanced at the beggars fighting for rotten food in the dustbins, and waved away the streets kids sniffing glue from empty milk pints who asked him for money at the robots. Hobos were also taking advantage of the many robots in town. Further along, the street hawkers spread out their products. Police tried to remove them, but they kept increasing in numbers. Macko continued, passing women carrying Checkers grocery bags on their way to the taxi rank.

"May you please drop me at the Itshokolele taxi rank?" said the mother.

"There is tight traffic on that side. We can't go there. I am dropping you here," Macko replied and pulled up, not waiting to see if she agreed.

"Taxi drivers are devils!" muttered the mother, gathering up her possessions.

"You should buy your own car!" Macko said, counting out her change.

The women exited, her children climbing out after her.

The bald man also got out, his phone still in his hand, smiling at it. Others followed him until Macko and Dodo were alone in the taxi.

"I am going to Tabola's office. He should stop this feud between us and the Gauteng Taxi Association." Macko's voice was suddenly firm.

"Are you really serious?" Dodo stared at Macko, then shook his head. "Count me out. I'm not going there with you. I'm afraid of your boss. Just looking at him puts fear in me."

"I am serious, man. I am going there right now."

"Macko," Dodo lowered his voice, "I advise you not to go there. What you are doing is dangerous. Or have you forgotten how many people he has killed? They will never arrest him. He has contacts in the police."

As always, the rank was busy. Taxis making ups and downs, new and old ones. Some of the taxi-rank officials were pushing an old taxi, fully loaded with passengers, to give it a start. Women were selling braaied and boiled mielies to the passengers. A young man stood next to them screaming, "Ten rand two socks!" Taxi marshals were shouting to call the passengers to the correct taxis. At the corner, there was a queue of people waiting for the chesa nyama. All kinds of music played from the different taxis. People thronged through the lanes, waving the exhaust from the taxis away from their faces.

Further along the rank, there was one quiet place. On the door of the brick building was written "Chairman: Mr M. Tabola". No one played music or ran around near that office. Even the hawkers kept their distance from the place.

"He knows we are afraid of him and takes advantage of that! I've had enough. I am going to speak to him," said Macko, opening his door.

"Rather go see him when you are calm. Wait for morning. Please, my dog," Dodo climbed out the taxi after him, stopped directly in front of him, and then bent his legs and folded his hands like a praying person. His Rasta hair coiled on his shoulder.

"Just because he is paying my salary does not mean he can do anything he wants about me." Macko pushed past Dodo, and set off towards the office.

"Macko! Please stop that!" Dodo was left on the pavement, staring after him. He stood for a moment, then closed Macko's taxi door and went off to do his work.

Macko entered Tabola's office without knocking. The man sat at his desk, a plate of meat and another one of porridge in front of him, a bottle of Coke next to him. He didn't lift up his head to look at his guest.

"Who are you, not respecting me like this?" he asked, his mouth full of meat.

Macko kept quiet. He watched the man stuff down a fatty mouthful.

"I am asking you, who are you?" Tabola said again, still chewing. "What do you want?"

Macko looked at him. As the silence grew, he felt the fear take hold of his body. His legs weakened and beads of sweat burst on his forehead.

Tabola hit the table, sending the food flying to the ground. He stood up abruptly, towering over Macko. "I said, what do you want?"

"Yesterday I almost died because of you," Macko spoke at last.

"It would have been better for you to die. We wouldn't recognise that you are dead. You are not important!" Tabola roared the words loud enough for anyone in the vicinity to hear.

"Please, stop this taxi-owner feud between us and the Gauteng drivers."

"Who are you to tell me this?" Tabola asked, his face contorting into a frown.

"People died because of you. People are dying because of you. You must start building a peace with other people," Macko's eyes were full of tears.

"Get out before I put a bullet in your head!"

"Is that what you trust?"

Tabola took out his gun. He pointed it at Macko. "If you try to disrespect me like this again, I am going to kill you!"

He grabbed Macko by the scruff of his shirt collar, and pulled him to the door. "Qhwa!"

A small crowd had gathered outside the office, attracted by the commotion inside. They stood whispering amongst themselves, asking what was happening. Dodo stood on the edge, shaking his head.

"It is me who is putting food on your table, for you and that slut of yours. If you don't want to work, just say it!" Tabola knocked Macko on the head. He flung open the door and threw him outside. The crowd jumped back, and Macko fell down on the concrete, catching himself with his hands. Silence descended on the taxi rank. Even the full taxis waiting to leave held still, the drivers watching from their windows. Macko felt heat rising behind his eyes as the traditional drums in his head returned, louder than ever. They filled the whole space, locking Macko into his own world. He covered his ears. He got to his feet slowly, then lurched towards the door where Tabola stood. The other taxi drivers stepped forward, grabbed his arms and pulled him back.

"I told you, my dog," said Dodo, leaning in and talking softly into his ear.

Tabola scanned the faces in the crowd. He lifted his gun and shot two bullets up into the sky. Bullet shells bounced off the concrete and echoed. People ran.

Three

Macko wiped the sweat from his forehead again. "Ouch, it is very hot," he said, changing gears and braking as he approached the hump in the road next to the Tshibollo Senior Secondary School, then accelerating again. He needed to lodge a complaint about the state of the road to the relevant department. But not today. Today, all Macko wanted was to get home. He shifted up to third gear, then glanced in the rearview mirror to see how many people he still had to drop off. Three. Two adults, and a child who was crying softly to himself. The boy caught his eye, staring back at him in the mirror in a way that unnerved Macko. He forced his focus back to the road. Changed gears, but forgot to press the clutch pedal. The taxi lurched, and the ignition died, everything grinding to a stop.

He swung round to look behind him. "That baby belongs to whom?" None of the passengers answered. They stared at Macko in surprise. Fine. He let it be. He laughed to ease his discomfort, then looked forward. Behind him, he could make out snatches of conversation.

"I respect the foreigners … but sometimes they make you wonder a lot. Where does this guy see a baby here?"

Macko knew the speaker without needing to look back again. He recognised the voice followed by a characteristic hand clap, then a soft whistle. Mantsha. Everyone in the taxi industry knew the man.

"He does not show at all, he is very fluent speaking Sesotho, more than us. But yes, if you listen carefully, you can tell by his accent that he is not one of us. He is a foreigner," said Nnini. Another one of Macko's regulars, she was an employee in the sewing industry. Everyone joked that Nnini could sew a piece of clothing while someone was wearing it.

"Please stop gossiping!" said Mantsha. "But we must tell him when he drives a nonsense!"

Macko started the ignition. It took first time, and the engine purred back into action. He glanced in the mirror, but the child he was sure he had seen was gone. He shook his head vigorously to try to shake out the crying sound that still haunted his ears. He forced his eyes back to the road. After a few blocks, the cry in his head faded to nothing. He felt a wash of relief, but it did nothing to cool him. His ears still burned with pieces of the passengers' conversations. He looked for the water bottle next to his feet, but found nothing. He eased his foot off the accelerator and reached down, feeling under the seat. Still nothing. He wiped his face with his T-shirt. He looked at the dark sweat stain on the shirt, thought of sucking on it, but stopped himself.

"Please leave me at short right," said Mantsha. He spoke with his big voice as always.

"Mr Mantsha, please be careful out there. This area is well known for the gang called Dihase. They are very notorious and dangerous these days," Macko said, while counting out loose change for him.

"Ha," Mantsha snorted, "I was a gangster before they were born. I can break their knees!" Saying this, he closed the taxi door with all his strength; Mantsha with the tough hands capable of panel-beating Maluti buses. Even his body said it: short, but well built, with muscles that now rippled in the sun outside. "Go well!"

Macko changed gears. "Mme, where are you going at this time of the day?" he glanced back at Nnini.

"Just past Manapo Hospital," she said, pointing with her finger, like they were already near the hospital. "Hei, stop the taxi, there are people wanting a lift!"

"No, during the day they wave me past, choosing better taxis. It is only now because it is late and there are fewer choices that they want me. Let them leave me alone. I am already knocking off. I am just taking you home," Macko replied as he accelerated past them. "Do you mind if I smoke?"

"Not at all, you may smoke. My late husband was a great smoker. If the other drivers are the ones who are taking us home, they don't us ask for our permission."

Macko lit his cigarette. He pulled on it for a long time, releasing the smoke slowly, like he didn't want to let it go.

The traffic had thinned and it was getting dark. He began to count the money he had made that day as he drove. He divided it into three parts. The money for the boss. His own money. The money for Rose.

Outside, a group of people raised their hands, trying to stop him, but he just flicked his headlights to show he was done for the day.

"May I please stop at the café and buy some soft drink?" Macko asked Nnini, already braking, not caring if he got permission or not. He pulled up at the side of the road and opened his door, then stopped. The café was already closed. "Fuck! What am I going to do with this bloody thirst?"

"Eish, I am really sorry about this, sir."

"Keep quiet with your pity!" Macko rubbed his head. "I went to Katlehong and fetched water just yesterday. There should be some left at home But I failed to get soft drinks."

"No! Our bloody government. Just listen, they say we have better service deliveries, but we are fetching water from very far, from other towns."

"If you could just remember where I should drop you, that would be a great help." Macko glanced at Nnini in the mirror. He wiped his face again, swallowed saliva several times.

When they arrived at Manapo Hospital, Macko stopped before Nnini gave him the signal.

"Please go a bit further. You know it is not safe to walk here any more," Nnini asked.

"You see now. This is what I really don't want!" Macko turned alongside the hospital. He was travelling slowly, his window down. His headlights illuminated a pair of eyes, and Macko jumped in his seat. A cat. He stopped the taxi, peering into the dark. "I helped you till here. Go well!"

Nnini paid her fare and left the taxi without saying a word.

Macko waved her off, but didn't pull away. He flicked the lights onto bright and watched the cat. The animal was still staring at Macko, and he stared back for a few seconds, hypnotised by the yellow glow. Then he turned up the volume on the taxi's sound system. House music blasted over the speakers. The bass sounded in his stomach, and he opened the windows for everyone to hear. He focused on the beats, trying to push the cat out of his mind. At last he pulled away, pushing down on the accelerator so hard he even scared himself. The road filled with dust that shimmered in the dark. Other cars gave way. Macko overtook those that didn't. He drove like something was pushing him forward. The taxi shook, a red blur in the dark.

Macko arrived home exhausted. He went inside, wiping the sweat off his forehead, and calling out his girlfriend's name. Rose didn't even greet him. She immediately started complaining about the back door, which had something wrong with the handle. Macko sighed, followed her to the door, and tried the handle. The door swung free on its hinges, inviting housebreakers. Macko wiped his palms on his pants as he walked back to the taxi to fetch his tools. He tried to work on the handle, then gave up, deciding it would be better to take the whole door down and install it from scratch. He unscrewed the hinges, swung the heavy wood down onto the ground. Using a screwdriver, he bored into the wood and made new holes for the handle.

Rose stood watching him. Macko glanced up at her. Her hair was a mess, ruffled up like the feathers of a chicken, her lipstick slightly smudged. He noticed she was wearing a miniskirt. Macko looked at her and felt his penis push against his trousers. He dropped his tools and stood, taking a step towards her. Rose retreated, but he followed her, stepping in close, gently cupping his hands around her arse. She giggled and he could see her eyes flare, but she pushed him away, straightening her skirt, running her hands through her unruly hair. "Finish your work first, and then wash." Her voice was curt.

After about an hour, Macko had finished fixing the door. He tested it several times, opening it and closing it like he was welcoming a stream of invisible guests. Through the open door, Macko could see clouds forming. The air was heavy. The smell of rain filled his lungs, offering some relief. He collected his tools and walked back to the taxi, remembering to collect the money he had left earlier in his pouch, well aware that Rose would expect her share. He returned to the house, shutting and locking the door against the weather, pleased with his handiwork. Then he went straight to the fridge. Shit, nothing drinkable. He slammed it closed, went to the water buckets. Nothing. He held one up, dropped it so it clanged across the floor.

"Rose! Rose! Where are you?" He walked through the house. How was it possible that all the water he had collected from Katlehong the day before was gone? "Rose," he called again. He returned to the kitchen, this time noticing that the water bottle he usually kept filled in the fridge was under the table. He reached for it, held it first to feel if it was cold, then lifted it higher. The bottle was light, empty. He held it to his lips anyway, drained the last sip. He felt almost tearful. Leave it, he told himself. He threw the bottle down and walked to the bedroom where Rose was waiting.

Her smile told Macko that she was ready for him. He smiled back, and she moved toward him. Their bodies touched, an intimate hug. Macko closed his eyes. Rose's naked body was warm. She slowly loosened three buttons of Macko's sports shirt, then he helped her by taking the shirt off. Rose's hands were on his belt, then easing off his jeans. They breathed heavily on each other.

They came very close to one another and kissed. A sweet perfume rose from Rose, and Macko started caressing her, stroking her hair, allowing it to pass through his fingers. He kissed her on the forehead, then shifted down to her neck and shoulders, moving slowly, as if they had all the time to do this. Rose started moaning softly. Macko touched her nipples very tenderly, then bent to suck them. Rose's moaning grew louder. He then went back up and gave her a peck on the lips, and she moved even closer. He heard her voice in his ear saying, "Go on." His boxers were down. He put his arms firmly around her, kissing her slowly, sucking her lips like a lollipop.

His body reacted, feeling the warmth and smoothness of his girlfriend's skin. His penis was up and hard. He touched her wet vagina and kissed her deeply until she started making "ahh, ahh" sounds. He then lifted her one leg up and slowly penetrated her. "Yes, babe!" Rose implored. "Harder, please, please…" Macko pushed harder and faster. He groaned. He took his penis out and Rose bent down, sucked it, taking her time. Macko touched her head, brushing his fingers through her hair. When he could no longer wait, he lifted her onto the bed. She opened her legs, and Macko entered her, missionary sex position."Ahh, ahh! Ahh, ahh!" she called, even louder than before. Her moaning made him push harder. The bed was shaking. Rose gripped Macko's body with her legs, then loosened, opening her legs wider. They flipped over. The sound of the bed got louder and louder. Macko pushed very hard and fast. "Ahh, fuck me! Fuck this pussy!" Rose screamed. He roared like a hungry lion seeing its prey.

He slept with Rose's head on his chest. Sweat dripped off their bodies, dampening the sheets.

Macko was woken by thunder shaking the corrugated-iron roof. Bright streaks of lightning illuminated Rose's naked body. He covered her with a blanket and stood up. His thirst had returned: more than just a tightness in his throat, it seemed to grip his whole body. He felt as if he hadn't had water in weeks. He ran his tongue over his lips, glanced at Rose sleeping, then left the room.

Macko opened the back door, admiring his handiwork again. The lightning had stopped and the thunder was a distant roll. He went back to the kitchen, fetched a cup and headed out. He was wearing only his boxers, but that didn't stop him. Who would be out at this time of night?

He stood under the rain, felt it splash against his head, wash down his face – momentarily blinding him – stream down his body. He opened his mouth and let the rain fill it, swallowing mouthfuls of water. He lifted the cup to fill it, raised it higher, spilling water down his arm. He swayed, righted himself and headed back towards the door. But when he pulled the handle, the door stayed stuck. He struggled with it – he had just fixed it, how could the handle have jammed again so soon? He set off round the front, then stopped.

A bolt of lightning lit up the sky. A man, standing to the right of his taxi. His first thought was car thieves: minibus taxis were an easy sale for them. Adrenalin floored his system. He started to run, but his bare feet slipped on the wet ground.

The man stepped forward. He was smartly dressed, old-fashioned clothes, the trousers and jacket and hat Macko remembered his grandfather wearing. He seemed barely wet, as though the water struck against him, but then streamed off.

"What do you want?" Macko heard his voice shake. His feet seemed to sink into the mud.

"You are needed in Mozambique. Your grandfather has passed away. You must go to take care of his inheritance. That inheritance now belongs to you. You must go and take care of all your relatives." The man spoke slowly. His lips seemed to take the shape of each word that passed them. After he spoke, he turned and disappeared into the black night.

Macko stumbled to the back door, and this time it opened easily. He heard Rose calling. “Macko! Macko! Is that you? Please, baby, fetch me some water. I’m so thirsty.”

Macko stopped, glanced outside the window. The cup was lying in the mud where he had dropped it. The rain had stopped. The man was nowhere to be seen.

Four

THE TAXI DRIVERS were collected outside, taking cover in the shadow of the office wall, standing, then sitting, shifting in their seats, and checking their watches. From time to time, one of them would rise and take a few steps as if to leave, only to return after checking to see if their taxis were full yet. Others stood, stretched, then sat down heavily again. They had long since lost interest in playing morabaraba and the craft games that had occupied them all morning. Next to them stood four empty Coke bottles.

Eventually some of them gave up. Seeing no hope of any more commuters, they bid the others farewell and departed in their empty vehicles. "See you tomorrow, gents," said Tshomane, already inside his taxi. Known to be stubborn, he was a difficult man who liked to fight. He was of average height with a light complexion. His head shone and his beard was sheared clean. He rubbed his chin, and settled himself, taking his gun out the makeshift holster of his trouser waist and concealing it under his seat before leaning his head out the window. "Macko, my little brother. Pass my greetings to your boss," he said, raising his voice so it carried over the old-school music blaring at full volume from the taxi's speaker system. "But tell him this thing of us going to Qwaqwa and coming home with an empty load is not good." He watched as his colleagues raised their hands, making sharp signs with their fingers, then drove off.

Behind him, the taxi marshals' voices echoed: "Here is for Bethlehem!" "That one is for Harrismith!" "Here is for Qwaqwa!" "That one is for Bergville!" The drivers paid little attention. They were buried in their passenger lists. They wanted to arrive at their destination before it got very late, but they already knew they were in for a long wait. There were few passengers and too many taxis. The sun was about to set. People were packing their stuff. Hawkers filled bags with unsold produce, and others pushed trolleys still loaded with stock.

By five o'clock, the sun was low, and the taxi owners started to talk.

"The passengers are not many, let's put together those who are going to Harrismith, Qwaqwa and Bergville," said one, scratching his big stomach.

"Huh?" said the driver who was supposed to take commuters to Bergville. "Do you think this thing of combining the passengers of Bergville and Qwaqwa will work? They differ too much," he said while scratching his face as if his newly grown beard had started to itch. After some discussion, though, the drivers ended up agreeing.

Macko listened to them for a while, then returned to his taxi. The door stood open, welcoming passengers who did not come. Inside it was quiet. The few commuters for Qwaqwa were already seated.

"I pray to God to help to see this taxi go," said one of the passengers. He was seated up front, his hands folded. The other passengers nodded. They stared out the window, their eyes following Macko as he did his ups and downs. He was running, weaving through the stationary taxis, collecting passengers headed to Harrismith and Bergville. Already, two passengers headed to Harrismith were approaching. They climbed in, speaking loudly in isiZulu. Behind them, four passengers from the Bergville taxi also arrived, slinging their bags through the open door. The Qwaqwa passengers made room for them, hearing the frustration in their voices.

"Yes, you are right, sir," said an old man from the back. "It is like there is a fight in here. If we could just arrive home."

"Yes, it's like things will be bad. When you are not used to these things, it's bad," another Sotho passenger added in a whisper.

Finally all the new arrivals were seated. Macko climbed into the driver's seat and closed the door.

"Bathini labantu? Kuncono ukuhlezi unabanye abantu abangama Zulu. Ezinye izizwe lezi! Kubukeka sengathi bangabokufika bonke lapha eMzanzi," said a Zulu man who had taken a seat next to a Sotho family.

"Kunjalo, bayanyanyisa. Bayekele kanjalo kodwa," added one behind him, trying to pack his bags in amongst the luggage of the Sotho travellers.

The complaining stopped. The passengers were all seated; at last they were going home. Macko was in his seat up front. Was he going to Qwaqwa or Bergville? He would see on the road. For now, the important thing was to get moving. He turned the key and placed his hands on the wheel. He hit the accelerator, started to turn the wheel, then stopped. It felt like someone was holding their hands over his, clasping them tight so he couldn't move them. He struggled against the invisible hands. Behind him, the passengers were shifting in their seats. They could see him writhing, could see the beads of sweat collecting on his head. To them it must have looked like he was fighting some kind of internal battle. Finally, the force released him and his hands flew up from the wheel. He sat panting, then clasped them into fists, bent and flexed his fingers as if trying to understand what had paralysed them. He wiped his forehead with one hand, turned back briefly to the passengers as if he had just been stretching, preparing his body for the long ride ahead.

Macko put his hands on the wheel again and blinked. It was strangely hazy in the taxi, misty like on long rides when the cold from outside meets the heat of everyone breathing inside. Suddenly the haze disappeared. Macko reached for a cloth to wipe the windscreen. As he ran it across the glass in circles, he heard a voice, soft and urgent: "You are needed at home. No one is taking care of your grandfather's inheritance. The inheritance is being wasted." The voice reached Macko's ears like wind blowing through the open window of a moving vehicle. But the taxi was still stationary.

Macko swung round. "Who the hell said that?" he demanded, his voice edged with panic.

The passengers behind him started to grumble. Had their driver lost his mind? The man next to Macko shook his head in disgust. He took out his headphones and put them in his ears. He turned up the volume, and the sound of his hip-hop music filled the taxi. Macko stared at him as if he was the one who had spoken. He leaned over and shook the man's shoulder, then bent his wrist to indicate to him to decrease the volume. The man didn't move, and for a moment things were tense. But then the passenger switched off his music and pulled the headphones from his ears. The taxi was quiet again. Macko revved the engine and pulled the taxi out of the rank. The passengers settled down, happy to be moving at last.

Traffic was tight, but Macko knew the roads of Gauteng like the back of his hands, and wove his way through. He entered this road and exited that road. He entered that road and exited this road.

He arrived at the petrol station to find it was packed with cars. All the lanes were full. Macko waited a little, then saw a free pump and veered towards it. There was no petrol attendant to help him. He looked at the dashboard. The clock read 6:00 am. He hit it softly several times with his fist. It did nothing except make the numbers blink. Macko sat staring at the numbers that read 6:00 am. He reached for his cellphone, trying to get a grasp on reality. It showed that the time was twenty minutes past seven, later than he thought. The darkness added to the truth of the late hour.

He got out the taxi into the cold night. The smell of petrol filled his nostrils and made his head spin. He crossed the concrete to the pump. He tried to pull the handle that operated the pump's nozzle, but it was locked. Again, he felt frustration at being unable to perform the action he required. He let go the handle and shouted to an attendant filling up a car across from him: "Sir! Pass me your key, time has gone!" The attendant looked at Macko, shrugged as if to say let him serve himself if he wants to, and threw the key in his direction.

Macko looked at it flying towards him through the sky. His eyes grew wide. Mid-flight, the key grew feathers and wings, a tiny head. He saw eyes, eyes with a fire in them, beaming into him. He took two steps back, jumped sideways, and then ran towards his taxi. He scrambled in, started the ignition, pressed the accelerator. There was noise and the smell of tar eating a tyre. He paid no attention to the passengers' grumbles. He headed for another petrol station in the vicinity, where he was forced into a long queue of cars that were not there for petrol only, but also to have their tyres pumped, oil checked, windscreens washed. He kept hitting his head with his hand.

"Eish, you may wonder why these people were not pumping their tyres and washing windscreens during the day," Macko said as he checked and rechecked his cellphone clock. Behind him, the Zulu passengers were speaking in loud voices. They sounded unhappy but neither he nor the other Sotho passengers understood their words.

At last Macko's taxi made its way to the front of the queue. He climbed out and fetched the air pump while the attendant filled his tank. He knelt next to the tyre and felt the pump twist in his hand as the pipe swelled with air. He went from tyre to tyre, each time kneeling to fill them with air. He asked for oil and for the windscreen to be washed. He went inside the shop and came back with three big cans of Red Bull He gulped down two of them, throwing his head back and feeling the sweet liquid in his throat. The after-taste reminded him of petrol. When he finished, he dropped the cans instead of throwing them in the dustbin. The attendant looked at him, and pointed towards the dustbin. Macko sighed and bent to collect his cans.

As he approached the dustbin, he heard the noise of crying. It rose softly but steadily and filled the air like a bad smell: "Kiri, kiri, kiri." Macko looked around: a child he thought, maybe one of the street children who populate central Johannesburg. No, the sound was of more than one voice. He kicked at the dustbin, and the noise of the cries increased. For a moment, he thought he heard Rose's voice amongst them. He stepped away, turned and looked behind him. The petrol attendant was staring at him. Unable to stop himself, Macko approached the dustbin. He stretched his neck, ready to run. One side of his heart wanted to open it, another side wanted to leave it, get into his taxi, and leave the petrol station far behind him. He finally lifted the handle with shaking hands. When he forced his eyes open, there was nothing inside. The bin was empty, not even a piece of paper. He stared into its abyss. The metal bottom was corroding. It smelled faintly of sour milk. He dropped the Red Bull cans next to the bin, ignored the attendant's shouts, and climbed into his taxi with its waiting passengers. He started the ignition without saying anything.

"Sir, will we get where we are going?" one of the Sothos asked. No one answered.

Macko fastened his seat belt and veered onto the road. He knew that during the long drives, the passengers rarely talked to each other. They just wanted to think of arriving. Macko kept curving, changing gears. He went down. He went up. Curving with the road. He knew the road as he knew himself. He knew where the potholes were, sudden holes in the tar that can cause a disaster to a car. He slowed or swerved to avoid them. He stopped at the robots. The robots of Gauteng cannot be dodged like the robots of the small towns. There are cameras in Gauteng. He left the city and merged into the freeway, increasing his speed. The taxi was really moving.

Most of the passengers were sleeping by now. The passenger next to Macko had put the headphones of his cellphone back in his ears and was snoring. When the taxi swerved one way, he swerved with it, his body touching the door. When the taxi swerved the other way, his body swayed towards the driver. Each time, his seat belt stopped him from ploughing into Macko.

Macko glanced at him, then back at the road,

moving only his eyes. One of the passengers was dreaming, talking aloud. "You are needed at home. You should go," he said while in deep sleep. Macko was startled, afraid that he was also sleeping. What home? Thababosiu, his place with Rose? Mozambique was not a place he tried to remember. For all he knew, his family there had been dead for years. He looked back at all the sleeping people in his mirror. He reached down and retrieved the remaining can of Red Bull, and drank it.

"Let me just turn on this radio. Maybe it will help me," Macko thought, pressing the buttons of the radio. He couldn't find a station. The radio hissed and popped. Eventually he found something and twiddled the knobs to catch the signal. The music seemed to come from far away. Not inside the taxi, but from outside, somewhere in the dark night. "When are you going home? When are you going home? When are you going home?" a voice sang. The tune was soft and haunting. Macko felt a wash of cold. He hit the off button. In the quiet, he could hear the sound of the wheels on the tar, air moving in and out his lungs. He concentrated on the road.

One of the passengers woke up and asked, "Where are we now?"

Macko jolted at the voice, then answered, "Only an hour and twenty minutes." He didn't know if the person who had asked the question heard his answer. The taxi was silent again. Macko stared at the road ahead. All he could see was the small patch lit by his headlights; the rest was darkness. He watched the patch bend and curve, and fought drowsiness. He opened the window. Hot air flooded the taxi. The heat surprised him – it was winter. The weather report had said there would be a low of three degrees.

The road curved, the patch swung, the heat filled his lungs. Suddenly the darkness was broken by flashing blue lights. He leaned forward, straining his eyes. Ahead he could make out a figure on the road, shining a torch. His heart sped up, his tiredness banished. Was it a road block? The police had been clamping down on taxis since the latest flare-up of violence.

His lights illuminated the police officer's face. It was Detective Baile. He slammed on brakes, and everything went black for a second. Behind him, the passengers were awake and complaining. Some had hit the seats in front of them, others hit each other. Some were holding their heads in pain. Others were holding their elbows and waists. "Itjhuuu!"

"What is happening now?" one of the passengers asked.

"My goodness!" another exclaimed.

Macko climbed out and stood on the tar in the dark. The road ran empty ahead of him. There was no police car, no blue lights. There was nothing. There was no one. He turned, checked the front of his taxi, but found nothing. He took a few steps forward, straining his eyes into the darkness. Then he saw it: a shape moving, a shadow.

"Baile?" Macko shouted. What did the detective want? Was he following Macko? Was he a suspect in Baile's investigation? Macko had to know. He swallowed his fear and followed the figure. It took him off the road. He was in a field now, moving between tall mielie plants. Every now and again, he could see beams of light. He crashed through the mielies, not caring about the crop. The lights disappeared, leaving him in the field in the dark. The mielies stood next to him, silent witnesses. If they knew anything, they were not telling.

Macko was about to push forward when he heard a voice from the road. The passengers had climbed out the taxi. One of them walked towards him: "Hehe, sir! Take us home before we beat you now!"

He walked back to them. Stalks and husks from the mielies clung to his legs. "Forgive me please, sirs! I don't know what is happening," he said, breathing heavily. He shook the husks and leaves off his pants, and climbed back inside the taxi. The passengers were still grumbling. No one slept again.

Shortly afterwards, they arrived at Harrismith. He dropped two passengers there.

Bergville or Qwaqwa next? Macko was supposed to find a solution. "Sirs, you have to decide yourselves. Are we going to Qwaqwa or Bergville?" Macko asked.

"Uthini lomontu?" one of the Zulus asked angrily.

"Thiya siya eBergville! Finish and klaar!" said another Zulu, more furious than the first.

"Who is the majority here? You see!" a Sotho man said.

"Yebo, sirs, here is the money to take you to Bergville," Macko said, giving the Zulu men a refund on part of their taxi fare. He left the Zulus at the garage at Harrismith. Insults flew. "You people are all devils!"

Macko continued driving, now heading towards Qwaqwa. His Sotho passengers were happy that they had outvoted the Zulus.

"They still think it is the time of Shaka!" said one of them, laughing. Everyone laughed.

Another one said, "They can rather go fall in hell!"

Macko looked at them in the mirror, shaking his head with a hidden smile.

At about fourteen minutes past eleven, they arrived at Qwaqwa at last. Macko dropped the passengers at the rank. Those who could afford it took special taxis home, and those who couldn't were left there. Macko told himself it was not his issue any more.

He started the taxi and drove in the direction of his house. He was cruising now, relieved to be almost home. As he turned the corner into his road, he saw a car he recognised. Tabola's black 4X4. What did the man want in his neighbourhood? He watched the lights of the vehicle curve, then disappear. He had had enough questions for one night. He thought of the figure on the road. Was it Baile? He remembered the voice telling him to go home. Thababosiu in Qwaqwa was not the home the voice meant, but it was all he had now. He could not go back to Mozambique. He went inside his house. He found Rose asleep in bed. Surprised she had not waited for him, he curled up next to her and slept.

Five

IT HAD BEEN ANOTHER long day. When Macko arrived home, tired and hungry, the puppy was waiting for him as usual, but instead of bounding towards him, it barked like he was a stranger, like it didn't know him at all. Macko closed the taxi doors. Bang! Bang! The puppy's ears were pinned back, and its body shook with the force of each bark.

In the house, Rose shook her aching head. She wondered what all the banging and barking was about. Her face twisted, then slowly relaxed as she stirred the porridge in the pot. The movement calmed her. She lifted out the spoon and walked to the window, where she saw Macko and his puppy.

"Voetsek, voetsek!" Macko was throwing stones, trying to ward off the male dogs that hovered on the perimeter of their property, beadily eyeing his female puppy. He didn't know how he knew the dogs were male – he just did. Something about their tongues, how they lolled. Something in their eyes. Macko knew that look. He kept throwing stones at the dogs. Eye-shining dogs. The dogs didn't move.

Rose opened the window. "Love, what is going on?" she asked.

Macko didn't hear her. He was focused on the dogs. On the stones in his hand. On hitting the dogs with the stones.

"Your noise is killing me!" shouted Rose.

Macko looked to the window, saw Rose, saw her eyes, angry eyes. He went back to throwing stones. The puppy was barking louder, running circles around his ankles.

Rose went out, hands on hips, and asked: "Macko, what are you fighting with?"

He pointed speechlessly to where he was throwing the stones. He said, "Dogs."

Rose looked. There was nothing. No dogs. The only dog was Macko's puppy. It had stopped jumping up at Macko and stood looking at Rose.

"Macko, are you insane?" she asked.

"I swear! There were dogs coming here," Macko looked around, checking that what he had seen was gone.

"This thing of yours is getting worse. I am going to take you to a shrink. I can't stay with a mad person," Rose turned and stomped inside. She was getting more worried by the day. At first, she had brushed off the comments she kept hearing about Macko's behaviour. Let people talk if they must. She ignored rumours that her boyfriend was mentally ill. But now she didn't know what to believe any more.

"No, I am not going anywhere. I am mentally fit, Rose," said Macko, following her into the house. He left his barking puppy at the door. It wanted to get inside. It always wanted to get inside. But Rose wouldn't give it a chance. Macko sighed. She told him she hated dogs with their shit.

Macko walked slowly, his shoulders heavy. He went straight into the small dining room. As he was about to sit, Rose said, "Please don't sit down. Do you see how you look?"

Macko didn't respond. Rose looked at him. His clothes were spotted with oil – from his jeans to his off-white dice jersey. He lifted a hand to wipe himself, but his hands were also covered with black smudges. His head was covered with dust. Maybe his taxi gave him problems during the day, thought Rose. Maybe it broke down, and he tried to fix it himself, to try and save money. Maybe.

Rose put on the first kettle and poured the hot water into the bathing basin. She boiled the kettle a second time and added the contents to the basin.

"Here is the bathing water!" she called.

Macko took his time. Eventually he went to the kitchen, but instead of collecting the basin, he unlocked the kitchen door and went out. He went to his taxi and tried to open it. The door wouldn't unlock. He tried again. Still it didn't open. He hit the door several times with his fist. His puppy came running towards him, barking again. Macko tried to nudge it with his foot, but it jumped aside. The puppy slunk away, nose to the ground. Macko sighed and went back inside.

"Bathing water is getting cold. I am not dishing out this food for you if you are not going to clean off that smelly oil first," said Rose, dishing for herself.

It took all his strength for Macko to lift the heavy basin. His muscles strained to their limit. He went to the bedroom, washed himself and changed into clean clothes. Clean blue jeans, a long-sleeved brown golf shirt, and not forgetting his maroon dice socks.

Refreshed, he joined Rose, who dished up for him. He ate like a hungry lion and asked for more, licking his fingers. The tablespoon was next to him, but he didn't use it, so Rose dished up for him until there was no food left. In the shining pot of sausage and tomato gravy, there was only a reddish colour left, a faint salty whiff of sausage in the pot. The colour was from the cooking oil that Rose had used to fry sausage and tomato gravy. In the porridge pot, only brown scrambles were left. Rose filled the pot with warm water and closed it with its lid.

Even though Macko had enjoyed the food, he couldn't look Rose in the eyes. Rose guessed that he hadn't made enough money for the day, meaning she wouldn't get her share. She didn't ask. She wiped up the little scraps of food that had fallen as Macko had eaten and put the dirty dishes in the basin.

"You'll find me in bed," she said, with her dissatisfied voice. The voice she used when she thought she wouldn't be getting her daily share from her boyfriend.

Macko just nodded, water in his mouth. He looked at Rose as she disappeared into the bedroom. He wondered what Rose's reaction would be. Her reaction to what? He stood up and walked around. He was thinking and thinking. He looked at his fingers, adding, subtracting, multiplying. Realising that his fingers were dirty, he went back to the kitchen and wiped his hands with a moist dishcloth. He remembered that he had left the money he made for the day in the taxi and went out to it again.

Rose could hear him opening the kitchen door. She covered her head with the blankets, afraid he would start with the banging and the barking again, and bring back her headache.

Macko got into the taxi, found the money in his pouch, and split it into three parts. For his boss – to deliver tomorrow. For himself – he pushed it into one of his socks. The third share was for Rose. He took it all and got out of the taxi, locked it again. The puppy was waiting for him. It ran after him and watched him enter the house with its sad puppy eyes. He left the taxi key on the fridge and went straight to the bedroom.

Rose took off the blankets that covered her head. She smiled when she saw the money.

He gave Rose her share, and put Tabola's share on the bedside table.

"Are you joking? Only one hundred for me today?" Rose sat up in bed, and stared at the two fifty-rand notes.

Macko didn't reply. He took off his golf shirt and his jeans. He looked at Rose to see if she was watching him. She pretended to be busy with her cellphone, smiling like she was reading her messages. Macko looked away. He slowly took off his maroon dice socks. In them was his share of the money: five fifty-rand notes. Two in one sock. Three in the other. He combined them in one sock.

Rose's eyes were on Macko. She smiled. She would take the money during the night when he was deep in sleep. Or early in the morning, when she got up first to make hot bathing water for him.

Macko folded his socks. He couldn't wait to take the money to the bank tomorrow as he always did if Rose didn't take it all. He glanced at Rose, but she was still looking at her cellphone.

"Love, you don't want to sleep tonight?" Rose asked.

"I am here. I was just sorting Tabola's money," Macko replied.

"But here is Tabola's money." Rose pointed at the bedside table.

"Oh, yes. I was just making some calculations," Macko stretched and yawned as he got in bed, not looking Rose in the face.

"Okay. What is wrong with you today?" Rose asked.

"Nothing. Nothing. I am fine."

"I am asking because you seem jumpy and uncomfortable. I am here for you. You can talk to me freely." Rose put her cellphone away and held Macko's hand.

"Just unimportant work stuff, babe. You know how our industry works. Just many uninteresting things for you."

"I've got time. Try me. I am listening."

"Well, today one of our taxi drivers resigned," Macko said.

"Why? In these times of poverty?" Rose was surprised.

"Yes, we are the slaves of the taxi owners. We travel these long distances. People are dying daily because of the violence, you know it. We earn peanuts. We have no insurance. Our lives are always in danger."

Rose shook her head, and felt a stab of pain. She said, "You guys are very fortunate. You shouldn't be complaining. There are people who long to be just like you. There are people who have nothing on their table."

"Okay, I hear you. But even Dodo is thinking about resigning," Macko added.

"Oh, come on! Dodo is a taxi marshal. You can't compare yourself with him. Do you even hear yourself?" The pain in Rose's head increased.

"Let's leave this, please. I see you are not feeling well. What is wrong?" Macko asked, feeling a wash of sympathy for his girlfriend.

"It's you who talk too much. Sometimes you think like a sissy."

It was Macko's turn to look surprised. "But it's you who asked me."

Rose brushed Macko's hand in reply. Macko felt

her touch and returned it. She moved her hand to his boxers, but his penis was unresponsive. That was unlike him. Maybe he was stressed.

Macko reached for Rose and kissed her. She took off her underwear and rolled onto her side, wriggling up and down, her bottom against the front of his boxers. Macko's temperature increased to match Rose's, and she felt his machine getting bigger. "Yes!" she said, turning to Macko. He held his machine in his hand. She went down like something was pulling her. She sucked and sucked. Macko sighed with pleasure. Rose continued to suck, enjoying his erection. She moved up, taking his penis in her vagina, moaning softly. She took the lead, balancing on Macko's body.

"Babe, I have something to tell you," Macko interrupted, but Rose kept moving on him.

"Yes, babe. I am listening. Oh, damn! I love your cock."

"I have reached a decision. I want to resign from the taxi industry," Macko announced. His machine shrank in Rose's vagina.

Rose pulled off him and knelt on the bed, her hands on her waist. She glared at him. "Where do you think we can get money? Will we pay the rent of this house with your shit?"

"Calm down. We can maybe go to your parents' house? And I can look for work there," said Macko.

Rose laughed. "Now you are being selfish. Instead of working hard so that you can marry me, and stop with this damn cohabitation."

"Hear me out! I beg you. This is for us," Macko tried to reach for her hand, but Rose jumped off the bed, pulling the duvet and blankets away from him. She threw them on the floor, leaving Macko naked on the bed.

"You are useless! Leave that job and see if there will still be an 'us'. My mother was right – I should never have found a foreigner." Rose took the bedding from the floor and stormed out. "Suit yourself! You want to live like this? You will live like this!" she screamed from another room.

Macko threw his pillow at the door.

Rose curled up on the couch, pulling the blankets over her head. She heard Macko's footsteps.

"Leave me alone! Don't you dare come next to me," Rose shouted, lifting the blankets and pointing a finger at him.

Naked, disappointed, Macko went back to the bedroom. He hunted for a sheet in the wardrobe, finding two towels and a sheet. He folded his knees and slept.

Six

ROSE STEPPED OUT of the bathing basin. She wiped her body with a towel and stood in front of the mirror. She turned to the side, looked at her profile. Her breasts were of the average size but tight – showing that she had never had children. She put her hands on her hips, then moved them to her stomach. She inhaled, trying to make her stomach flat, but as soon as she breathed out, it protruded again. Not flat, but also not that big.

Average, she thought. She sighed. She tried hard to diet, but sometimes she couldn't help herself. She liked to eat when she got lonely. It wasn't easy to diet when Macko was always on the road. She told herself her stomach was his fault. She rubbed her hand across the smooth surface, then breathed deeply and pushed her stomach out. She smiled at her reflection, admiring herself. She pulled her eyes away from the mirror and looked downwards. Her stomach looked bigger from above. She held it in both hands and rocked back and forth. "One day is one day, my girl." No, no, not a girl. A girl will run after sex to get money, not taking care of me, her mother. "To you, my handsome boy."

Outside, Macko's puppy started barking again, shaking her back to reality. She exhaled and watched her stomach and the baby disappear. She looked through the window to see what the dog was barking at, but saw nothing. Turning back to the mirror, she looked at herself from head to toe. She looked at her big arse. She swung her knees back and forth, and watched her bum shake. She liked to wiggle it at Macko when she was horny. But Macko wasn't Macko at the moment. Maybe he was tired. It didn't bother Rose that much.

She poured the water from her bath into the bucket, and wiped the floor dry with an old brown facecloth. It had been Macko's until Rose bought him a new one. She thought if she hadn't bought it for him, he'd still be using the old one. He was like that. He would wear a thing until it was finished.

Rose slipped on her panties, lifting each leg and pulling the elastic up around her waist, snapping it against her stomach. She put on her pink dressing-gown, not minding her loose breasts.

She carried the water outside, and poured it next to the toilet. The puppy ran after her, jumping at her legs. "Voetsek! I am not one of your family. Voetsek!" She waved the bucket at it. Instead of it running away, it started sniffing her feet. Rose kicked at it, and the dog snapped at her, growling in its throat. She let out a shriek, dropping the bucket as she ran towards the house and slammed the door.

Her phone sounded, an incoming SMS. She checked it and smiled.

She went to the bedroom and opened her wardrobe, taking out some of her favourite clothes, a mix of dresses and jeans, as well as some of her sexy lingerie, and putting them on the bed. She picked up a maroon dress that did not cover the knees. She held it at arm's length and looked at it. It was the dress she had worn on her first date with Macko. She brought it to her nose, smelling the cotton, and pressing it against her body. She remembered Macko's first touch. He had opened the car door for her and taken her smoothly by the hand. She also remembered the high heels she had worn that year. That month. That week. That day. That night. They were also maroon. She dropped the dress and crawled under the bed, looking for them. She found only one shoe from the pair.

She sat on the bed with the shoe in her hand, remembering that day at the Zee Lounge. It had been a beautiful evening. A beautiful time. They had laughed together. They had ordered the same food. Joseph Dee's "The Smell of the Rose" had taken everyone by storm that night – Rose and Macko were drunk on it.

They had met only recently, by chance. Macko was buying lunch in a store where Rose and her mother did their grocery shopping. He volunteered to push the trolley for Rose, then to take her home. He asked her to dinner. Rose was nervous at first. She had been through a series of bad relationships.

But as soon as she saw Macko that night, her anxiety disappeared. They had talked about children. Macko said he wanted four. Rose laughed. They talked about how they both wanted to find someone special and get married. Now it was over three years, and he still hadn't popped the question.

Rose put the dress back in the wardrobe and threw the single shoe back under the bed. She didn't want to think about Macko now, but there was no escaping the memories. Everything in the wardrobe carried traces of him. She touched a dark-blue jean skirt, and remembered how shy Macko had been to kiss her at first. She had taken the lead. She remembered leading his hand up her skirt, spreading her legs so the denim pulled tight. His hand sliding into her panties.

Rose clasped the skirt tight and touched her lips. Then she shook her head and pushed it back into the wardrobe.

She looked at the time. The clock was ticking. She crossed her arms at her waist, looked up at the corrugated-iron roof, and looked at her clothes again. She picked up a yellow designer skirt with its matching top. Macko had bought it for her on her birthday, with his last money. Rose threw the yellow two-piece outfit aside and took a dark-pink, full-skirted sexy dress instead.

She took off her dressing-gown and panties. Now she was completely naked.

Her phone rang in the kitchen, where it was charging. She ran to it, her big bum shaking. As she was about to answer, she saw the caller was Macko. She put the phone down again and watched it as it rang. It didn't want to stop. Eventually it was silent, but Macko called again immediately. Rose held her cheeks in her hands, her elbows on the counter. She bent her curvaceous body, sticking her bum out. She checked the time again, left her cellphone, and went back to the bedroom.

Rose forgot which dress she wanted to try on next. She grabbed her white jeans. Slid into them, pulling her stomach in to do up the button. It was one of her favourite pairs, they really showed off her body. But as soon as she let her breath out, the button popped open. Meaning she had gained weight. She took the jeans off. "Maybe I am better without any clothes. After all I am going to be naked in the end anyway," she said to herself. She picked and picked at her clothes, setting them down, losing interest.

As she was about to give up, she saw the dark-pink, full-skirted sexy dress again. She remembered that she had been about to try it on when her phone rang. She pulled it over her head and admired her reflection in the mirror. She was beautiful. Even her heart said so. She turned and turned as she looked at herself.

A memory clicked. Her mother had bought her the dress, as a bribe. Immediately after she had paid for it, she told Rose not to make the mistake of marrying a foreigner. She said that all taxi drivers were useless, and asked Rose to dump Macko. According to her mother, he was not earning enough, and would never be able to take care of her properly.

Rose got angry that day. She nearly threw the dress back in her mother's face. Her mother told Rose that there were many men on this planet, and she could organise some muti for her to get a rich man.

As Rose was a Christian, this made her even angrier. "No, Ma. You know that is against my belief."

"What does your belief say when you sleep with someone you are not married to?" her mother asked. "Don't tell me about beliefs!"

Rose had dropped the subject with shame in her eyes. Deep down, she knew that her life was wrong according to her own beliefs. A tear came as she remembered that incident. She came back to reality and wiped her eyes with the dress.

She stood looking for sympathy from the mirror. "Rose, you are strong. Calm down and live life as it is. Life is rotten, why worry about it?"

The cellphone rang again and she ran to it. "Ag!" It was Macko again. She left it ringing, went to the dining room, and put on a soul song to get her in the right mood: Teddy Pendergrass's "Hold Me In Your Arms". She smiled. Whether it was fake or not, at least she now had a smile. The dimple provided some happiness.

Rose went back to the bedroom. She looked among her clothes. She chose a red miniskirt and tried it on. She felt fabulous in it, confident. For the top, she picked a tight pink blouse.

She remembered she had some purple lingerie she liked a lot, and went hunting for it. It was not among her other clothes. She looked on Macko's side of the wardrobe, taking out all his clothes. The smile on her face when she found her lingerie hidden on his side was big. She danced a little stripper's dance to celebrate: slowly on her way down, and slowly on her way up. She kissed the scraps of lace, put them on the bed.

The puppy barked outside. Rose hurried to take her chosen outfit off. She smeared herself with a perfumed body cream and put on her makeup. She changed her mind about her purple lingerie – there was no need for any underwear. She slipped back into the red miniskirt and pink blouse. She put all her clothes back into the wardrobe, stuffing them in, not bothering to fold them. She changed the duvet, and put a clean cover on. She changed the pillowcases. The room was sparkling. She went to the CD player in the dining room and changed the disk to one by Boyz 2 Men: "That's Why I Love You."

She heard a car outside. The puppy barked. Rose went to the window, looked through it. It was just a passing car. The puppy followed it as far as the corner. Rose left the window. She lit candles. She braided her glossy hair and slipped on a pair of blue-red high heels.

Another car stopped. She knew the sound of the engine. It was a black 4X4. The shining shoes emerged from it first: Tabola's shining shoes. He was carrying a bottle of sparkling red wine. He wore smart black trousers, crisply ironed, with a fashionable black shirt. His face matched his clothes. He took his black sunglasses off, and looked around. He put them on again, then came to the door to knock.

Rose rushed to the door. She smoothed her skirt, licked her lips, then opened the door with a smile. The puppy came running, but it was too late. Tabola was in. He gave Rose the wine. Slid five hundred-rand notes into her cleavage. Rose touched the swelling in his pants. She turned, pulling Tabola by his trousers. He put another five notes in her waistband and slid his belt off, leaving it on the floor. They went to the bedroom. The music continued to play.

Seven

MACKO STOOD ALONE, two ten-rand notes in his hand. He waved them as if to cool the air. He looked at a group of passengers with big bags who were going to the long-distance rank. He wondered about the money he would have made that day if he had taken a long-distance trip.

There was a question on his mind. He kept trying to push it away, and it kept jumping back. Why did Tabola allow him to get off from taking the Gauteng trip that day? He knew his boss liked it when he took the long-distance trips, even if he was only transporting seven passengers in the fifteen-seater Quantum, even if they were not making any money out of the trip.

"But maybe his holiday to Durban beach changed him into a better person," Macko thought, yawning, cupping his mouth with his hand.

It was around ten in the morning and quiet. Most of the old and regular hawkers were still arriving at the rank and constructing their stalls with different materials. Plastics. Sails. Hardboards. Other opened small containers: public phone booths they had taken over. Others opened their small municipality-built rooms. Most people called them the toilet stalls, as they fitted only one person at a time.

Even the taxi marshals were quiet. They were saving

their voices for when it was busy. Macko watched the passing passengers, following them with his eyes. Suddenly he was still. Not blinking. The two ten-rand notes stopped waving. Only his heart kept beating.

A middle-aged lady approached him, coming from another taxi driver, who pointed her towards Macko.

"Good day, sir," the lady greeted. She had put something white all over her face. Maybe it was a calamine lotion for rash or pimples.

There was no answer from Macko.

"Sir, please help me with change," she said.

Again, Macko did not respond, even though his eyes were looking right into the retinas of the lady. "I am going home!" she shouted. She dropped the big bag she was carrying and waved her hands in front of Macko's eyes. He did not blink. "Is this man alive?" she cried. Other passengers had turned, and were staring.

A man's voice broke the quiet: "Sister, we are going without you, it is getting late! We are going home!" The words came from the driver of the taxi who was taking passengers from Qwaqwa to Newcastle in KwaZulu-Natal.

"Sir, we are going home! I need some change. Please give me those two ten rands. Here is a twenty-rand note in exchange." She held it out to Macko, but he did not reply. He kept clasping his ten-rand notes. Then he blinked, his eyes caught by something moving in the big bag belonging to the lady.

"What is that?" Macko asked, pointing at the bag.

"We are going home! It is late!"

The lady snatched the money out of Macko's hand, and pushed her twenty-rand note between his fingers. Macko looked at the lady's face, and felt a cold flush spread through his body. He felt itchy, and his hands started to shake. He kept hearing, "We are going home!" The words looped in his mind.

"I am not going with you!" Macko said, surprising even himself with the force of his voice, the anger it contained.

"I didn't ask you to! Thanks for the change." She took one ten-rand note over to some boys who had helped her to carry the bag to the rank. One of them was holding a pint of yellowish glue. Then she picked up her bag, ran to the taxi, and climbed in. The engine roared and the taxi turned to the exit.

Macko could feel sweat running down his face. His shirt was wet. It clung to his body. He shook his head, brought his hands up, and held it. He squeezed his temples. His breathing slowed. He looked around the rank. Some people were staring at him, some not. In his head, the words kept playing: "We are going home! We are going home! We are going home!"

His eyes followed the taxi. He wanted to see the lady's face one more time. The sun was shining on the window, making it hard to see. He blinked again. Instead of her face, he saw the detective, waving, calling to him. He started to back away, almost tripped over the fruit stall behind him. Two apples rolled free from one of the boxes. They looked very red against the concrete. The fruit seller ran after them, glancing furiously at him before rubbing them on her skirt and dropping them back in the box.

Macko suddenly felt tired and hungry. He crossed to his taxi. He stood at the passenger door, looked into the taxi, his eyes adjusting to the darkness inside. There was only one empty seat. He looked at the seated passengers, his eyes travelling from face to face. He opened his mouth. His lips felt cracked, his tongue swollen. The passengers stared back at him, waiting for him to speak, but he said nothing, simply closed his dry mouth.

His stomach growled loudly, overcome with the craving for a plate of braaied meat. He slammed the passenger door of the taxi, and turned towards the mothers manning the stalls. He forced himself to walk past braai-ing meat. The smell of it filled his nostrils, but he didn't stop. He went to a woman who sold maize and cow's legs. Next to her sat a fat woman selling mielies – raw, boiled, and braaied. Macko stood before her, and before he could ask for maize, she stretched her hand up for money. She pressed her eyes, making them smaller because of the smoke billowing up from the braai-ing maize. She was waving the smoke away with a torn piece of hard box. Macko coughed. He blinked against the smoke and handed her twenty rand.

"You want which one?" she asked, small eyes, mucus coming from her nose.

"The braaied one." Macko pointed, averting his eyes from her and towards the braai.

"A full one or a half?" she asked, opening a metal container that kept the maize hot.

"How much is a full one?" Macko asked, his eyes still watching the fire dance and the maize sizzle, its edges slowly turning black.

"Twenty!"

"Give me a half," Macko said, needing to get change.

The fat woman reached into the container. She pulled out a mielie, pressed her thighs tight together and pursed her lips to get the strength she needed, then broke it exactly in the middle with her bare hands. She dropped the broken mielie into a small plastic bag and gave it to him with a small sachet of salt. It was red, carrying the KFC logo. Macko chuckled as he took the salt – either the fat woman had a salt sponsorship from KFC, or she was stealing the sachets somehow.

"My change, please," said Macko, tearing opened the sachet.

"Ag, you are one of the stingy men," she grumbled before handing him ten rand.

Macko didn't respond.

The passengers in his taxi were growing restless, and some wanted to get another taxi. Dodo had to beg them to stay before heading off to find Macko fighting with a half-cob of maize. Dodo ran back to the taxi, with Macko following behind, too tired to run. The mielie hadn't touched sides, and his stomach was still growling.

"Taxi drivers will always be taxi drivers," said one of the disgruntled passengers.

"Ja, they will always be shit. All of them!" added another, glancing at his watch.

"Just look at that dirty dog!" said a passenger, pointing at Macko trudging towards the taxi.

Macko sighed as he opened the driver's door. "Hello, good people," he greeted the passengers. None of them replied. He looked at them in the mirror. They did not look happy.

Dodo, who was standing to one side, washing a mat belonging to the vehicle of another driver, called after him: "My broer!"

"But I give you lifts." Macko shook his head, then gave him the ten-rand note.

Dodo smiled.

Macko changed gear from neutral to first and pulled out of the rank. He took the main road. It wasn't busy, but numerous roadworks fixing and patching potholes slowed the traffic. Macko stopped at one of the Stop & Go signs. "After this, they are going to make mountainous speed humps," he said, shaking his head. No one even coughed. You would swear he was alone in the taxi.

"May you please combine your taxi fares according to your seats and pass it to me?" Macko demanded

The road workers opened the way and stopped the oncoming traffic. Macko was able to drive on. Behind him, the passengers gathered their money and handed it forward. He counted it while driving. Slid the notes and coins into his pouch. He dropped three passengers at the short left. He took out his cellphone and SMSed. "Hi babe. How are you? Are you enjoying Durban with the other girls?"

"Bus stop!" Two passengers spoke at the same time.

Macko was staring at his cellphone. Without checking the traffic behind him, he turned into the bus lane, almost hitting the side of a bus just pulling out. The bus's hooter filled the air. Macko managed to slip in front of the bus and park. He blew out his breath. Most of the passengers didn't even notice the near-miss.

"At least I am out of this taxi. I am not ready to die," a passenger grumbled, gathering his bags and heading for the door.

Macko wasn't listening. He was looking at his cellphone. He tapped out another SMS. "Babe, take some beach pictures and send me, please." Message sent and delivered, his cellphone declared.

He glanced at his phone one more time before sliding it onto the dashboard in front of him. He was out on the open road now, heading towards the village. He put his foot down and watched the black tar ahead speed towards him.

He reached the turn-off and dropped two passengers at the corner. The remaining passengers wanted to go into the village, and he dropped them all next at the big kraal. The smell of cow shit filled the air.

Macko breathed deeply. He looked around. He saw the valleys full of streams. The pale grasslands shimmered, and he remembered how green they were in summer. The place reminded him of the village he grew up in. The birds on the many trees sang songs he missed. He found himself smiling without knowing why exactly. The girls with firewood on their heads greeted him. One of the boys herding the cattle ran to stop a cow from crossing the road. Macko remembered the smell of wet earth and cows in the early morning when he was growing up. Before the soldiers came. Most of all, he remembered the sounds of water in the valley. He used to throw stones in the river, and loved to watch them jump across the water, breaking the surface into spiralling rings.

Within a matter of minutes he was out of his taxi, almost racing to the water's edge. Standing, looking, then bending to scoop up a handful of stones. Without thinking, he lifted his arm, sent a stone skimming across the water. He jumped with joy and glee. Realising that he was fully grown, a man not a boy, he stopped, looking around to see if anyone was watching him. The distant herd boys were laughing at him, but he didn't mind. The laughter reminded him of the children he used to play with. The noises they made when they were jeering. He remembered the melodies of the birds. His grandfather always summoned him and his friends to chase them away from his crops. He saw the mango trees and remembered shaking them so that the fruit would fall. Collecting and carrying it to his grandmother, who would make chutney. He swallowed his saliva. He thought about the spicy sauce she made with chillies and ginger. The butter bananas she cooked in coconut milk. The cow that got sick from eating a plastic. They slaughtered it and invited all the people from the community to come and eat. At that time, people brewed a traditional beer – pombe. Or they made a strong liqueur from pineapples. They ate and drank. It was very relaxed in the village. No loud unnecessary noise. Peace ruled. Neighbours' sympathy ruled. Sharing was the thing that connected the people. When others had no maize-meal for chima, they would ask or borrow from their neighbours.

"I can find a place here; it is not bad at all," he thought. He took few minutes to look around before going back to his scrap and driving off. He stopped at the edge of the village and waited for the cows to pass before turning. He drove slowly back to town, dreading returning to the noise and smells of the taxi rank.

He picked up his phone, his eyes flicking from it to the road. There was still no answer from Rose. He was held up in the queue at the Stop & Go again, but he didn't notice the wait. His mind was on his cellphone. He called Rose, but there was no answer. After twenty minutes, the road was opened, and he could thread his way through the patched potholes.

He arrived at the taxi rank, where the atmosphere was much livelier. Different music from different radios welcomed those who were arriving. The smell of chesa nyama was stronger. Macko smiled and touched his pouch when he smelled it. He had money. Forty rand for a plate was nothing to him. He parked next to a dustbin where two mad people were fighting and digging for food. Taxi marshals shouted on this side, shouted on that side. A group of young girls was singing and dancing next to the entrance. Taxi drivers were happy to see them, as they kept throwing money towards them. Not just coins, even notes. People with groceries in their hands were headed to the different taxis. They came from different shops, the plastic bags different colours. Yellow. White. Red. Brown paper ones. Young glue-smokers helped some of the people carry bags to the taxis.

Macko parked, and Jim, one of the popular taxi drivers who always wore a woollen hat, even in summer, stopped next to him: "Boss, to be honest with you, you look like hell. Did you sleep yesterday?"

Macko glanced at his cellphone again before turning to Jim: "That funeral made me tired, boss. Take me seriously when I say that child is haunting me."

"But I heard that you did not even hold a single spade. You need to go home, and rest. I thought I saw your twin ghost in the morning." Jim continued, revving his taxi.

"Fok, which twin ghost now! It was me you saw. You know, the taxi violence in Gauteng is getting worse. They don't want to see FS number plates." Macko yawned.

"Eish, boss. You should try local. You once worked here. You are champ. Go home and tell your madam to massage you. You know what I mean by massage." Jim laughed.

"I wish she was around. She is in Durban. I am trying to contact her there, but she does not respond," said Macko, his eyes going to his phone again.

"I'm sorry about that. Did she go alone?" Jim asked.

"No, with some girls. Her friends," Macko answered.

"How sure are you? Did you really see her friends?" Jim laughed again. "Boss…" he paused. "We will talk very soon. I should warn you." With those words, he sped away.

Macko watched him drive off, wondering what he meant. He got out of the taxi, and followed the smell of the braaied meat. He checked his cellphone one more time, but it was silent.

Eight

MACKO STRETCHED HIS BODY to slide open the big passenger door. But Mantsha shook his head. He wanted to sit next to him, next to the driver. He ignored the open door and climbed in on Macko's left.

"Hey, brother!" Mantsha greeted.

Macko kept quiet.

Mantsha stared, then stretched across, grabbed his arm and shook him. "I'm greeting you, man! What, did they badmouth me to you?"

"Stop, Mr Mantsha. I am fighting with money here. I am at work." Macko's eyes were busy, searching for the passengers.

"Eish, you guys and your taxis!" Mantsha looked at the back. His eyes settled on a schoolgirl in a dark-blue uniform, her dress taken up into a miniskirt, showing her plump yellow thighs spread across the seat.

"You were once a driver, Mr Mantsha. You should teach us how to make money. Anyway, are you going to work at this time?" Macko asked, holding the steering wheel with one hand, glancing across at Mantsha.

"Yes, I was off, but on standby. I got a call to say one of the buses has broken down. But remember, I drove when there were not as many taxis fighting for such a small number of passengers." Mantsha looked back again. The girl was staring out the window. He looked at Macko, but Macko was still looking for the customers.

"When it is not the month-end like this, we don't make money at all," Macko said. His eyes fell on the sign pointing the way to the Bolata village. He slowed the taxi, then stopped for a moment to see if anyone was looking for a ride. He hit the hooter several times.

"But Macko, today I am brave to ask you. Are driving locally or long-distance trips?"

"As you know, I'm meant to be driving long-distance. I'm just waiting for the taxi feud to cool off, then I'll start again," Macko answered politely.

Mantsha shook his head. "You never cease to surprise me."

Two people were approaching the taxi. A mother and her son, hands clasped together. Their feet kicked the stones on the ground as they walked, causing dust to rise around them.

Macko sounded his hooter again, hoping to attract them. The hooter was loud enough to be heard through the entire village. But the woman and child didn't even glance up. They passed the taxi and kept going. Macko clapped and pressed the hooter for a minute. "Dammit! This is the taxi industry for you. I wonder why they did not shake their heads to show that they are not intending to ride this taxi."

"Then they will say taxi drivers are stupid, while they are also stupid!" said Mantsha consolingly.

Macko changed gear and moved on.

"I am very sorry about that, hey. Don't worry, you will find another passenger." The voice came from behind the men. It was the schoolgirl. She spoke slowly and her voice was soft.

Macko glanced in the rearview mirror and found the schoolgirl giving him a sexy smile and slowly rubbing her thighs. Macko blinked. He turned his head to look at the girl, and found her opening her thighs. He saw something black. He coughed and swung his eyes forward. But in seconds, he looked back again. The girl was not wearing any panties. Macko coughed again. Mantsha glanced at him, frowned, looked at the girl, then forward again.

Macko thought about the darkness between the girl's thighs. For a moment it felt like it was calling him, a huge black hole that wanted to suck him in. He swallowed hard. He could feel one of his headaches coming on. "Kutu kutu! Kutu kutu!" filled his head, then dissipated. He shook his head, tried to concentrate on the road, on making money.

"Please drop me at the clinic," said the schoolgirl as they were about to pass the small brick building.

Macko hit the brakes. "Little sister, did you pay me?"

"Yes, I did," she replied quickly.

"When? I've driven you from Letshalemaduke, and since then I haven't collected any money in this taxi." Macko was very serious.

"Oh, yes. You are right. I forgot. I am really sorry." She dug in her bag, found a ten-rand note, and gave it to Macko.

Macko said nothing. He inhaled deeply. He exhaled deeply. The girl closed the door, and walked towards the clinic gate.

"Then they will yell at the poor taxi drivers, telling that they all come from the same vagina!" Mantsha shouted. The young girl paused, obviously hearing the words, but she did not look back. She entered the clinic, swinging her arse like a famous model.

The taxi moved on.

"These girls! And you won't believe me when I tell you that they do this every day. It's like they belong to one mother, as if they tell each other what to do." Macko hit the hooter as he passed a shopping centre.

"I wish I was still a driver." Mantsha smiled. You could see that he was thinking about it.

"And if you were still a driver?" Macko asked with a half-smile.

"I would never get hungry." They both laughed. "Ei, wait! That Palestinian is stopping us."

The taxi came to a halt.

"Going to town?" the Palestinian asked. His hands were filled with stock: three big plastics of snacks, a plastic of stock sweets, a box of biscuits, a carton of Peter Stuyvesant, another of Dunhill, one of Craven A, and another of Courtleigh. A bag of Boxer tobacco. A sack of oranges. Macko stretched to open the passenger door, as it didn't open from the outside any more. He had been stretching like that since yesterday, and his body was starting to feel it. His back was sore. Macko rubbed it while waiting for the Palestinian to settle in his seat. Mantsha moved his own seat forward to make the Palestinian more comfortable.

"Mr Mantsha, these girls, they just want sex and money. You see she is going to the clinic, maybe she is going to get contraception, or even abort. You never know." Macko looked back to see if the Palestinian had settled. Yes, he had. He was leaning back, breathing hard. The cartons he carried made Macko crave a cigarette. "Sir, you can pay me with a box of cigarettes," he said, only half-joking. The Palestinian just smiled a little and looked out the window, avoiding Macko's eyes in the mirror.

Macko set off again. Some empty taxis passed him. Others had two or three passengers. Those who knew Macko greeted him by flicking their lights. Others hit their hooters.

Mantsha continued their conversation: "When I got in the taxi, I thought she was your mistress."

"I have no time for girls. I want money, that's what I need. Having many girls is expensive." Macko's head was out the window, looking for passengers.

"That is true. But lately, these girls have huge curves, they are fitter than their mothers."

They both laughed. Even the Palestinian joined them, laughing loudest of all. Macko and Mantsha both glanced back in surprise, not expecting him to understand them.

"Drop me here. I am going to fix that bus." Mantsha pointed to a bus by the side of the road, its load of passengers standing on the pavement with worried looks on their faces. He handed Macko his ten bucks and disembarked.

Macko went on. He was near town now. Still no luck finding enough passengers. He hit the hooter again and again. He saw a group of people standing near the robots. Three women – teachers, he guessed – just finishing at the school. He knew they'd need transport to town. In the rearview mirror, he noticed a taxi coming up behind him at high speed. It changed lanes, aiming to pass on the left. Macko pressed his accelerator hard. There was no way he was letting the rival taxi take his passengers. The robot was green. It changed to yellow. He pressed his foot flat. The robot was red. He was going too fast, there was no way he could not stop even if he wanted to. He sped through the red light. And immediately saw a traffic officer's car behind him. He slowed down, but too late. Behind him, a siren sounded and the flashing of blue lights filled his mirror. He had no choice but to stop. The other taxi sped past him and then pulled over for the three teachers.

Macko hung his head. There was no point protesting. Even if he didn't admit his fault, the street camera would have captured it.

The traffic officer wore big black sunglasses and a cap. He approached the taxi and stood at the window writing on a small pad. Macko started to say something, then stopped himself. It would probably be better for him to hold his tongue. The officer tore a sheet out of the pad and handed it to him. Macko stared at it. A fine for R750. Shit. Macko closed his eyes. He was imagining what Rose would say. She didn't understand how hard it was on the roads, and was always blaming him when he got tickets. He turned to the traffic officer, ready to plead his case, then stopped. The officer's face was in shadow. He could feel himself being pulled towards it. He heard a voice. Was it the officer?

"What? I'm sorry..." Macko started.

This time, the officer's words were distinct. They echoed in Macko's head: "Go home." With that, the officer turned and started heading back towards his vehicle. Macko stared after him. His feet seemed to glide, like there was a space between them and the ground. Macko watched as the man reached his car and drove away. The siren was dead, but the blue lights were still flashing. They swirled into the distance.

Macko brought his hands to his face. He pressed his palms against his eyes, rubbed them. Behind him, he heard the Palestinian shifting in his seat, and that brought him back to the present.

He started his taxi and went on. In three minutes, they were in town. He waited patiently for the

Palestinian to get off with all his stuff. The man bent to check under his seat, making sure he hadn't dropped anything. Then he paid Macko and waited for his ten rand change. Macko handed it to him. The Palestinian pushed the door open, and next thing it was down on the ground with a loud bang and dust rising around it. Macko held his head. "Kutu kutu! Kutu kutu!"

"I am very sorry, sir. I didn't mean to break it," the Palestinian pleaded, raising his hands, looking like he might cry. Macko saw his eyes pause on the sign on the door asking passengers not to be angry at it. The Palestinian hung his head. It was obvious he felt guilty.

Macko breathed deeply. After a few minutes, the drumming in his skull disappeared. He climbed out of the taxi wearily. "No, my brother. It is not your fault. Go in peace, I'll fix it." His voice was calm. He picked up the heavy door, wincing as the pain shot up his back. He tried to slide it back into its slot, but did not succeed. The Palestinian guy helped him to push harder. The door caught in the groove. Macko went to the back and fetched a hammer. He pounded the door into place. The red paint was now badly scratched. The Palestinian went on his way.

Macko climbed back in his vehicle and drove back to the rank. The queues of the taxis were moving very slowly. After an hour, he realised that he had no chance of getting a load. The sun had already gone to rest. Perhaps he should go to the panel-beater. The man was an old friend of Macko's. He knew he could count on him to help, and that the man would let him pay when he had the money.

It was a short drive. Macko found his friend busy with some old bakkie that needed his attention. Macko waited. He tried to chat to his friend as he worked, but the man's mind was clearly occupied, focused on the bakkie. Macko watched him hammer and wished he had a skill like that – anything but driving. The street lights came on. Finally he got in his taxi and left for home.

He pulled up in front of his house and sat counting his money for the day. Only three hundred. He subtracted it from the costs he had incurred – the R750 fine and whatever he would have to pay for the panel-beating. The day was a failure.

He locked his taxi and walked slowly towards the house. He was hungry and tired, but he did not look forward to facing Rose.

She was in the kitchen cooking when he entered. He kissed her on the neck, then went straight to the dining room. He watched the news, trying to take his mind off the day's events. Rose brought food and they ate together, the television still blaring. After eating, Macko pushed his plate away and dozed off in front of the TV. He tried to keep his eyes open, but kept yawning, then nodding off. Rose got irritated. She took the dishes to the kitchen and went straight to the bedroom.

Macko followed Rose. He sat down on the bed, took out his money, and put it on the bedside table.

"Where is my share?" Rose asked with her eyes on the cash.

"Today it was very bad. It was worse than other days. You will get it when there's enough, my darling," a sleepy Macko answered.

Rose crawled over to Macko who was sitting on the bed, taking his shoes off. She hugged him as he untied his laces. "Babe, our neighbour bought a washing machine and a tumble dryer. Can you buy me a washing machine and a tumble dryer?"

"Babe, we don't have that kind of money, as you see. You cost me a lot when you were in Durban.

Besides, did you ever use a washing machine and a tumble dryer in your life?"

"Listen to your mouth. According to you, I am not smart enough to use them? You are just a useless man! Some men work very hard every day for their families!"

Macko quickly stood up. "You just said I am useless?"

Rose also jumped to her feet. "You give those schoolgirls money. They are your sluts!"

"Shut up, woman! You are insulting me!" Macko pointed a finger at Rose. He approached her.

Rose backed away. "You don't reserve my respect!" she wailed.

"I said, shut up!"

"You want to beat me? You want to beat me? Go ahead! Your cell is waiting for you!" Rose screamed.

Macko stopped. He held his hands over his head and sat down on the bed. After a few moments, he climbed under the covers.

Rose stood whimpering. After it became clear that Macko wasn't moving, she climbed in next to him. He faced one way, she the other. They did not even touch each other's backs. Neither wanted to switch off the light. It kept burning. Eventually they fell asleep.

Just before morning, Macko tossed and tossed, mumbling. A giant animal, something like a gorilla with no head, came crashing into his taxi. He tried to fight it, to save his passengers, but he could barely move. All his joints were weak. He couldn't stand or speak. The giant animal killed everyone in his taxi. Then it approached him. It held him by his neck, and threw him down hard. As he was about to hit the ground, he woke up. He was soaked in sweat and gasping. He lay still for a moment, then fell back asleep.

In the morning, Rose woke first. She kissed Macko. He kissed her back even though he was still half asleep. He opened his eyes cautiously, not sure whether the dream had gone. Rose reached down and slid off his boxers. Macko tried to move his body, but everything hurt. He stopped kissing Rose. Feeling the pain, he turned over, facing the other direction. Rose sighed. She lay looking at Macko's back, then got up. Macko heard her put on the kettle. He felt her climb back to bed. She brushed his chiskop. "I am sorry for fighting with you yesterday." Macko didn't hear. He was snoring again.

Nine

Only one more person, and then the taxi leaving the Wanderers rank in Johannesburg would be full. Passengers who were already in the taxi kept their eyes on the people passing by, hoping they were also going to the Free State. People came with bags: "Is this taxi going to Rustenburg?" Disappointed, the passengers shook their heads. "Is this taxi going to Witbank?" others asked. Again, the passengers shook their heads. They eyed another group of people – but no, they were selling things. Expensive items at a discount prices. Things like gold watches and small DVD players, Nike and Adidas sneakers, Guess and Levi's jeans. Some of them appeared to be second-hand. Others were very new, fresh out the box. Most of those who sold these things checked the surroundings before they opened their bags. They whispered to their customers, always willing to negotiate a discount, asking how much money they had. Most of the passersby ignored them.

Macko stood at the rank offices, looking at all the paying passengers crowding into taxis. "I wish that money was mine," he said quietly. The lady helping the passengers at the counter, a woman by the name of Sarah, didn't even look up at him. She was known for not taking any nonsense from any man. A deep scar under one eye told a story, a story that made men fear and respect her.

Macko watched passengers come and go. His face lit up when a passenger going to the Free State arrived: "I am going to Qwaqwa." It was a thin old man who kept coughing.

"It is R140, old man!" Sarah said. "Why don't you put your hand on your mouth? We don't want to get infected by whatever disease you have." She took his money by the tips of the notes: a hundred-rand and a fifty-rand note.

"My child, respect your elders," the old man said, hefting a big bag with a broken handle in one hand and clasping his walking stick in the other.

"You must respect yourself before we can respect you!" Sarah shouted. "Here is your change, now go." She gave him a ten-rand note.

The old man took his change, and waved his stick at Sarah: "I'll smash you now! Show me some respect."

She backed down even though she knew that the iron bars between her and the crowding people wouldn't allow the stick to reach her, and said, "Okay! Okay, old man! I have work to do, as you can see. Please go. I really don't have time for you." She kept taking money from other passengers.

Then she called, "Hey, old man! You didn't give me your address, including the address where you are going, and your contact numbers."

The old man returned to the counter. "I come from Thokoza, I don't remember the address. I am going to Qwaqwa. There is a beautiful village there with green…"

"Just the name of the village and your contact number, please!" Sarah interrupted him. She closed her eyes when he coughed again.

"Its name is Mononotsha. I don't have a cellphone, but take this paper. On it is written the number of my older daughter." He handed her a piece of dirty paper. Sarah took it and wrote down the number on it.

"Where is that taxi?" the old man asked politely.

"Wait for me outside, I'll take you to it," Macko said. He didn't mind the old man, as long he was going to where Macko was going. He stepped over to Sarah, who was calculating the money. Macko also calculated it to make sure. Sarah took her fee, and gave Macko the rest. She also gave him his passenger list.

"Arrive alive," she said.

"Thank you. Today I am going to sleep at home. Take care. See you."

"What do you mean? You slept here yesterday?" Sarah asked as she went on helping passengers.

"Yes, my taxi had only one passenger, and it was very late."

"Ah, you should have told me!" Sarah gave him a naughty smile.

Macko laughed and went out. He met the old man outside, and together they went to the taxi.

"Here is the taxi, old man," said Macko. The old man nodded, spluttering then coughing again. This time he held his mouth. Macko noticed that some of the seats were empty. He read a list, "Sello Chabeli?"

"I am here," Sello responded with a loud voice.

"Maki Dlamini?"

"Present," Maki responded quietly.

"Paballo Nkgatau?"

"Yebo," said Paballo.

"Mokete Mofokeng?"

"Here!" Mokete responded confidently.

"Tankiso Miya?"

"Sure," Tankiso responded.

"Dimpho Motaung?"

"Also here," Dimpho spoke with a shy voice

"Setjhaba Mokoena?"

"I'm going," Setjhaba responded.

"Sebolelo Mohapi?"

"I can't wait for this taxi to go," Sebolelo said, with a big grin.

"Morwesi Rathulo?"

"Eita!" came the reply.

"Thembelihle Mabombo?"

"I miss home," Thembelihle responded.

"Sibongile Tshabalala?"

"I'm also here," said Sibongile.

"Motlatsi Molaba?"

"Super!" Motlatsi responded.

"Lesiba Mosifa?"

"I'm with you," the old man coughed.

"Thabang Molefe?"

No one answered.

"Mohau Twala?"

No one answered.

"Can somebody please tell me where these two people are?" Macko asked. No answers came. "You see now!" Macko got in the taxi and started the engine. Waited for five minutes, wondering about the two missing passengers. He looked at his list and saw their cellphone numbers. He immediately called them: "Guys, you want to sleep here? Or will you go home walking?"

"Sorry, sorry, grootman. We are coming." Within two minutes, they arrived. They found their bags outside the taxi, smiled, boarded quickly. They were young, around fifteen years old. "We are here, good people. I am Thabang Molefe and this is my friend Mohau Twala." They opened their eyes wide.

"You smoke nyaope?" Macko asked, not expecting an answer. "Get in the car." They took their seats, still smiling at everyone. Macko loaded their bags into the back. Sipho, a well-known taxi marshal in Gauteng, helped him. Macko gave him some coins, then climbed back into his taxi. The old man had taken the front seat next to him. He glanced at him, then put his hands on the wheel. It was exactly one o'clock. He had managed to get a full load of passengers early for a change.

Macko stopped at the first garage, pulling into a vacant lane to fill up the petrol tank. He got the oil, water. Washed window-screen. Pumped all the tyres. He started the taxi again, hit his indicator and turned, taking the left lane that joined the highway. The young passengers who had boarded late were still smiling. Every so often they broke into laughter for no reason. Macko kept glancing back at them. They made him nervous. Finally he saw they had fallen asleep, their heads drooped forward and their mouths hanging open. Macko focused on the road running out in front of him. He put his foot down all the way to the next stop.

When the taxi arrived in Reitz, a few passengers got out to buy some food. The sleeping youngsters whom Macko suspected had been smoking nyaope were not moving. People pushed past them in order to get out of the taxi. Others jumped over them. Most of the passengers opted for fish and chips. A few preferred Russian and chips. The Portuguese shop always kept fast food warm because they knew the taxis would bring hungry passengers. A few complained that the Portuguese food wasn't fresh, and headed in the direction of KFC. The taxi filled up again. The smells of different foods filled the air. People ate. People drank.

Two people had been dropped off in Reitz, so there was now a bit more space. Passengers quickly filled it, using it to put their food down or spread their legs.

When they were back on the road and things had settled down in the taxi, Macko turned on the radio. The voice of the announcer filled his ears. "South Africans are demanding that all illegal immigrants return to their countries of origin. There have been reports of threats towards foreigners." It was quiet for a moment in the taxi. Macko kept driving.

"This thing of wanting to kill the foreigners is not good at all. God does not like it at all," said the old man.

"Whether God likes it or not, foreigners must go back to their different countries. Otherwise we are going to kill them." The boy who had earlier identified himself as Thabang Molefe spoke loudly.

"I am glad I am finally going home. Everyone must know his or her home, especially in times like this one." The old man looked at Macko, who kept quiet. "The problem with us, especially men, is that we sometimes abandon our own families, forgetting our own people. Leaving our traditional roots behind."

"Where do you come from, old man?" Macko asked.

"I've been living in Thokoza for almost forty years now. Not once visiting my original home. I wonder if they will still accept me. I was a police detective many years ago," the old man said.

"You've never contacted your family?" Macko asked.

A woman's voice came from the back. "That is why Father's Day is not important, not necessary at all. You fathers, you men, you like to abandon your families." There was real pain in her words.

"But not all the fathers. And there are even mothers who do that," said the old man, coughing. "Yes, driver. I never contacted them."

As the conversation moved, the taxi moved. Soon they found themselves in Harrismith. They stopped and dropped off five people. Now they were nearly at their destination.

"And you must know that in abandoning your family, you hurt many people. You take the hope of many people. You kill their feelings, their hearts, without realising." The eyes of the old man were full of tears.

"Where is your home, young man?" he asked Macko.

Macko took time before answering him. After ten minutes he said, "I don't know where my home is."

"Everyone has a home. What do you mean?"

"I was not born in South Africa. I came here after I managed to escape the military of my country when I was seventeen years old. I was taken and trained as a soldier when I was thirteen years old. My parents died when I was six. After that, I was raised by my grandfather, who is a farmer – if he is still alive," Macko said.

The taxi arrived in Qwaqwa. They dropped off four people, and headed straight to the rank with other passengers.

"Hei! Stop! Stop!" Thabang, one of the sleepy youths, now awake, screamed and made a lot of noise. The passengers looked at him in surprise. Macko pressed the brake pedal. All the passengers lurched forward – luckily their seatbelts were fastened.

Thabang raised a hand. "Driver, you were supposed to drop us at the bus stop. Take us back or give us our change, we paid in full."

The passengers were tense except for Mohau, the other youth, who was still snoring.

"Mohau, my brother, wake up!" Thabang shook Mohau, who startled awake. "Where are we?" he asked. He raised his feet before raising his body. "Where are they taking us?"

"Young boys! This taxi won't go back, I am going forward," Macko said.

"Then we are not going anywhere," said Thabang with stubborn pride. Mohau nodded, agreeing with his friend.

"Please push me to hell!" Macko shouted.

The boys shook their heads, refusing to leave the taxi. The old man opened his door and got out. He quietly opened the passenger door. People wondered what he was about to do. He seized Thabang and Mohau. Although they were bigger than him, he grabbed them like feathers and threw them on the ground. "Ouch! Ouch!" they cried. They didn't say anything further. Macko and the other passengers looked at the skinny old man in surprise as he threw out the bags belonging to the boys. Then he got back inside, and Macko set off again without saying anything.

In less than two minutes, they reached their destination. All the passengers disembarked except the old man.

"Listen here, young man." The old man tried to get Macko's attention, as he watched the passengers collect their belongings. The last one to get out closed the passenger door. It was getting dark, and there were very few people at the rank.

"I am listening, sir."

"I want you to listen to me very well."

"Okay, old man."

"You need to go home. You are needed in Mozambique."

"Wait. Wait. I did not tell you I was from Mozambique. Where did you get that I need to go home?" Macko demanded. He stared at the old man.

"Who the hell are you? How do you know my home?" He was angry and scared at the same time.

The old man ignored him. He got out of the taxi, turned and waved his hand.

"Wait," Macko screamed. "Wait, your bag! And your stick. What am I going to do with these things?"

Macko reached for them, but the items weren't there. He looked back at the old man. He saw nothing. Just the long dark shadows cast by the overhead lights of the taxi rank.

Ten

IT WAS MORNING. Macko was standing next to a twenty-one seater taxi, destined to take commuters to the Wanderers rank in Johannesburg. The taxi belonged to Macko's colleague, Jim. There were only two passengers in the taxi so far. A middle-aged man in a dark-brown beret slumped in his seat. He wore a golf shirt with a brown collar, a light-brown dice jersey, and Brentwood trousers. Crockett & Jones shoes were shining on his feet, white dice socks clearly visible. Maybe he was going to collect money from some Gauteng firm.

Next to him, a girl was absentmindedly clicking her black ballpoint pen. Her ears, enclosed in headphones, didn't hear the clicking. From time to time she answered her cellphone. "I also miss you, my boo. I can't wait to see you for the first time. Talking to you via WhatsApp is not ayoba – enough for me." As Macko walked past the taxi, she smiled, her long artificial eyelashes flicking up and down.

The next taxi from Qwaqwa was due in twenty minutes. It left at around seven in the morning. Macko saw that the taxi next to him was also far from full. He looked down, kicked his shoes against the pavement, tired of watching the owners, who could afford to buy soft porridge from the mothers selling it. He could hear their murmured appreciation: "Not these cornflakes I eat at my home. I was raised eating this, and I will die eating it."

"Tell that to your wife!"

They all laughed while enjoying their hot, tasty porridge.

Others were buying braaied chicken feet with warm vetkoek. Others preferred their vetkoek with mango atchar.

Macko felt his stomach rumble and turned his attention away from the food. He focused on the radio blasting from the nearby taxi. He hoped to hear the driver's report, which announced the situations on different roads: broken robots, accidents, traffic jams. At last he stood up from the plastic chair he was seated in. Rose's words that morning were still running through his mind. As he took a step, two drivers rushed to the empty chair, falling over each other until one managed to plant his bum down on the seat.

"Our association should buy us chairs, not worsen the violence of the taxi industry," Macko said as he walked away. He went to his own red taxi. There was no vehicle behind him, so he could reverse out of the rank. He wanted to do a round or two in his scrap, transporting commuters locally, to get time moving while waiting for the twenty-one seater to fill up.

He collected a passenger headed to the end of Qwaqwa, in Tsheseng. It was a mother, a fat woman, holding three plastic bags. She shut the door hard. A second passenger waved down the taxi. It was Nnini, the woman who sewed, who often rode with him. Today she couldn't open the door from the outside. Macko had to balance the brake pedal and stretch his body to open the passenger door from his seat. But as soon as she settled, Nnini asked to be dropped at the nearby veld.

"Are sure you want me to leave you here?" Macko asked. She nodded without speaking, and Macko dropped her in peace. Glancing back in the mirror, he was surprised to see her standing on the road, lifting her hand to stop another taxi. He shook his head. He hit his hooter, eyes searching the road for commuters. After a two-minute drive, he picked up another passenger, a young nurse who wore her blue work uniform. She sat, then immediately pinched her nose tight with her fingers.

Macko looked at her in the mirror. "Nurses – hygienic people," he thought.

The taxi kept passing people and other empty taxis, going in the opposite direction. They reached the end of Macko's circuit, a small, village clinic and dropped off the young nurse. "Please close the door carefully," he pleaded, and the nurse slid it shut instead of slamming it. After she got off, Macko tried to find the source of the smell that had bothered her. He turned his head around and sniffed. Nothing. His shoulders relaxed.

As he steered the taxi back onto the narrow tarred road, he suddenly smelled it too: a cloying foul odour. He tried to cover his nose with his hand, but the smell seemed to have penetrated his skin. His hand was of no use. Maybe the smell was coming from outside? He glanced around, trying to see if any of the windows were open. Yes, two of them were open, near the fat mother. She had probably opened them.

"Makhulu, may you please close those windows."

Without saying anything, she reached her hand across and slid the windows shut, but the smell remained. Macko thought he must be imagining it. He told himself that there was no smell, but his senses refused to listen to him. In fact, with the windows closed, the smell was getting worse, costing him his concentration. He only spotted a passenger when the man whistled as the taxi passed him. Macko hit the brakes, slid into reverse gear, and backed up. He balanced the brake pedal and again stretched his body to open the passenger door. The young man got in.

"Sho, kakapa. I thought you are not riding with me any more," he said. He was carrying a car battery.

"No, my bro. I was just busy with something," Macko said.

The young man turned his head: "Oh, sorry, Makhulu, I didn't recognise you. How are you?"

"I am fine, ngwana ka. It is good to see that among today's youth there are still some of you who greet elders," she replied. "May the Good Lord bless you, my son."

The youth started to cough. He wrinkled his nose, nodded with a fake smile. Took off his dirty blue top and put it to his nose. Macko realised he was not imagining the smell.

"Please drop me at that old parked van," the young man asked. He paid his taxi fare and went off with his battery. "Ke a leboha," he said, after getting his change.

"This boy is well-mannered. He knows how to greet the elders, and he knows how to thank," the fat mother said, clapping her hands with happiness.

Macko smiled. They turned onto an untarred road.

"You'll drop me next to that big kraal," the mother pointed.

Macko stopped the taxi. The fat lady took her time opening the door. She struggled with her three plastic bags. As she picked them up, the rotten smell rose. Macko frowned.

"You see, I am supporting you. You should also come and support me by buying my malamohodu – animal's tripe," she said, as she took out a hundred-rand note and paid with it. "After I have washed them, you will eat and eat deliciousness."

"It is still early, I don't have enough money," Macko responded.

"Okay, you'll get a discount when you buy this meat. Let me tell you, I also sell muti for people like you. I know these taxis make you drivers not perform well in bed, as you spend most of your time sitting, like now. You need to service your kidney. Ke a leboha."

Macko watched the woman walk away, bags swaying next to her.

Macko turned near the kraal. As he reversed, he felt a bump. The taxi slid to one side, stalled. He could hear the wheels spinning in the sand.

"Voetsek!" he said. He climbed out and surveyed the damage. One wheel was stuck in a deep hole.

"My boys! My boys! Come and help here!" Macko turned and saw the fat lady, still holding her bags. She shouted and waved her arms, and three men appeared. The lady pointed them towards Macko's taxi.

The men were carrying cups made from baked-bean tins in their hands. They set them down to the side as they approached. "These little guys don't know how to drive!" said one of them.

They pushed while Macko pressed the accelerator. The taxi shuddered, then jumped free. One of the men approached the window and said, "Give us something to buy another pint of this," pointing down. Macko saw the cup he referred to. Something brownish swirled in the bottom: moqombothi. A bad smell rose. Macko gave him ten rands in coins. He didn't wait to see what the man did with the money.

He turned back onto the tar road and rushed to the rank. He didn't stop for passengers. His mind was on Jim's twenty-one seater. Maybe it had filled and left. In no time, he was approaching the rank. He pumped the volume on his radio. He didn't want his mind to have space to stray towards Rose's words that morning.

"A middle-aged woman was killed early today in Johannesburg, while she waited in line for a taxi at the Wanderers taxi rank. The woman was gunned down and three people were seriously injured when a gang fired shots at 8:30 am. After randomly firing shots at the crowd at the rank on the corner of Wanderers and Noord Street, the five gunmen fled on foot. The shoot-out was believed to have been linked to the taxi violence." After this announcement, the DJ played Mzwakhe Mbuli's "God Bless Africa".

Macko arrived with the music blasting to find the rank wrapped in silence. It was like everyone had been told to be quiet in order to hear the news bulletin on the radio. The twenty-one seater was full by now, but Jim told Macko that Tabola had given the order that there would be no taxis to Gauteng.

"The taxi industry will never be a good place. It is built with blood," one of the drivers stated.

"Where is Tabola?" Macko asked.

Jim lifted his hands: "I really don't know."

Macko took out his cellphone. Tabola's phone rang and rang. The taxis to Gauteng had to be cancelled as the big boss instructed. But where was he? No taxi to Pretoria. No taxi to Vereeniging. No taxi to Johannesburg. Commuters were given their money back. Most of the taxi drivers who were supposed to go to Gauteng were happy.

"The taxi industry will never be a good place, because it is built on the blood of innocent people.

That blood will always wake up and fight to kill others," the same driver stated again.

A group of drivers whose taxis were cancelled didn't waste time. They went straight to the Matima Lenyora Bottle Store and bought beers. Macko thought about going home. Rose's words jumped in his mind. No, he would rather do another local round. That would keep him busy.

He rounded and rounded. He did three rounds with a full taxi. He opened the door for all the passengers, balancing the brake pedal and stretching his body from his seat. It was tough. He was tired and sore. It was enough. He decided to go home and face what he didn't understand.

Macko arrived home before sunset. Rose was not surprised. She knew everything from the horse's mouth. Macko found her busy on her cellphone. He wasn't interested in who she was talking to, or what they were talking about. He went straight to the bedroom and threw himself on the bed. He closed his eyes.

Rose followed and sat next to him on the bed. She brushed his head with her hand. "Babe, we need to talk. Like serious talk."

Macko didn't move. He pretended he didn't hear.

"Babe, please wake up. Let us talk." She shook Macko.

Macko opened his eyes. "I am listening."

"I have reached a decision. If you don't want to see a shrink like I asked this morning, I am moving out. It is over between us. I am helping us here, not you only. Seriously, you have been behaving so strangely. Even at your work they have noticed." Rose's face was serious.

"You know I have to work. My boss won't

understand that," Macko said. He turned and looked at Rose.

"Forgive me, but I had no choice. I asked him. He said it is okay."

"What? When did you talk to him?" Macko sat up, hit the wall with his fist.

"Babe, please don't scare me. I am helping you here. I didn't give him the details." She clasped her hands and gazed at him with teary eyes. "I asked him today while he was still in Gauteng."

"Tabola is in Gauteng? Why is he there? Did he have anything to do with this morning's shooting?" Macko asked.

"Babe, please leave that. Let's talk about going to see the shrink," Rose begged.

"We will have to hire a car, babe," he said, lowering his voice. "I don't have money right now."

"Your boss is going to lend us that other taxi, and Jim will use your scrap for work," Rose said.

Macko stood up and looked at Rose. She didn't lift her head as she waited for an answer. He turned his back. He held his head with both hands and rubbed it for a while. Eventually he agreed. "Okay. We will go before the end of this week."

Rose jumped up and hugged him. "We are in this together."

Eleven

MACKO PRETENDED TO SLEEP, but he could not. Would not. His mind was on the trip ahead, his appointment. The night seemed to crawl. He opened and closed his eyes, hoping to see a clear sky. To deal with what lay ahead.

For once, Macko was up before Rose. His appointment was in Jagersfontein, and they left at around four in the morning. They didn't talk. It was a long and silent trip. The road was bad, and Macko had to concentrate to avoid potholes. Rose stared out the window like she wasn't there, or dozed. After four hours, they arrived exhausted.

"I thought this Jagersfontein was a better place," Macko said. He looked around. It was a town of white buildings. Old ones. Cracked ones. Old whites were sitting on their stoeps or driving their old cars.

Rose sighed. "Let us go inside."

They got out of the taxi and Macko locked it. Rose took his hand. As they crossed the road, something in one of the trees caught Macko's eye. Movement, feathers. It was an owl. The tree was tall, bare branches, a scattering of leaves. The owl's eyes followed him, and he stared back at the bird as if it was talking to him.

The door to the doctor's office had a sign on it

saying, "Open. Push." Rose pulled Macko by the hand and pushed the door. They entered and were greeted by a friendly sounding woman. "Welcome to Dr du Toit's counselling service!" she said with a big smile. "I'm the receptionist here. My name is Mary. Please follow me." She led them to the next room, a waiting area.

"Doctor will be ready to see you just now. Please feel free to call me if you need anything, I'm just there," she pointed to her desk in the other room. Rose and Macko sat quietly, too nervous to talk. The receptionist's phone buzzed, and she answered it.

"All right, doctor. I'm bringing them now," she said, and hung up the phone. She went to the waiting room, the smile still on her face. "Doctor is ready to see you. Please follow me."

Maybe she was always smiling, thought Macko. She knocked at the doctor's office door and opened it without waiting for an answer. "Please go in and take a seat," she told them.

"Good morning, Mr and Mrs Ndawu," the doctor greeted them. He too wore a smile, along with a dark-blue jacket with a sky-blue checked shirt.

"Good morning, doctor. Thank you," Rose smiled, liking that the doctor had mistakenly called her Mrs Ndawu.

After a brief pause, Macko also said, "Good morning, doctor. Thank you."

"Whenever you're ready, tell me what brings you here," the doctor said, taking off his jacket. "Remember, the only person who can tell your story is you. Let me also remind you that you are the expert on your own life. I am not here to judge you. My job is to simply listen."

"Uhmmm, doctor, it's Macko, um, Mr Ndawu,

doctor … my husband here has been behaving weirdly lately," Rose started. Macko glanced at her, then returned his eyes to the doctor's face.

"All right." The doctor leaned forward over his desk. "Mrs Ndawu, could you please give me some time alone with your husband?"

Rose stood, uncertainly. She looked at Macko, and he nodded. She left the office and went back to the waiting area. The receptionist smiled at her as she took a seat. Rose smiled back, but the smile sat tight on her lips. She sat with her knees together, thinking of Macko alone with the doctor. She wondered what he was telling him. She looked down at her knees and waited.

Dr du Toit listened quietly as Macko spoke. He interrupted only occasionally to ask a question or clarify something. Macko spoke in bursts at first, then everything began to pour out. He spoke about the little boy he saw shot in the taxi violence. "Blood sprang like water from a tap. That poor child." He wiped his eyes. "Doctor, I am from Mozambique. I lived in a village, but when I was thirteen, soldiers came and took me. They made me fight. I walked in a pool of blood. That is why I hate my own home. I don't have a home any more." At last he ran out of words and sat looking at the doctor.

The doctor smiled again. He told Macko that his problems could be resolved, but they needed to discuss treatment options. His voice was cool but reassuring.

"Would you like your spouse to be here to hear the treatment plan?" Du Toit looked at his watch.

"Anything is fine with me."

The doctor picked up the phone on his desk, "Mary, please ask Mrs Ndawu to come in."

They two men sat in silence. Macko looked at the crumpled tissue in his hand.

"Macko, you are needed at home."

He lifted his head and stared at the shrink. The man's eyes had disappeared. His glasses were still on, but behind them black holes gaped. Macko jumped back in his chair, his heart racing in his chest as he began to pant. His hands were shaking. He was about to get to his feet when Rose and the receptionist entered. Macko swung his eyes from them to the doctor. He started to speak, but stopped himself. Du Toit's eyes had returned to normal.

"Mr and Mrs Ndawu, I suggest we continue with these sessions. Please make an appointment for next month." The doctor looked at Macko. His voice was calm and reassuring again, his eyes kind. "Your anxiety is completely understandable considering everything you've been through. The important thing now is to start to deal with the trauma you have suffered. We will do this in our therapy sessions. I have no doubt you will recover fully. In the meantime, I am going to prescribe some medication to help with the anxiety."

"It's going to be fine, babe," Rose took Macko's hand and squeezed it.

"Please excuse me, I'm rushing somewhere," Du Toit said as he picked up some files on his desk and ushered them out of his office.

Macko's heart was still beating fast. A wave of confusion washed over him.

"But Rose..."

Rose put her finger on his mouth, "Let us go, babe. We are finished here!" She turned, and Macko had no choice but to follow.

"Let's go get the prescription, and then we can celebrate, my love," Rose said, tugging at Macko's hand.

Macko shook his head. The doctor's words were

ringing in his head: Macko, you are needed at home. Macko, you are needed at home. Macko, you are needed at home. He felt weak. He let Rose pull him outside.

Twelve

MACKO ATTEMPTED TO stay awake by moving his head from side to side, drumming his fingers on the wheel. Rose brushed the top of his head. He squeezed his eyes shut and then open again. The soft evening sunset made the air shimmer. Ahead of them, the road swung in a sharp curve.

Rose's eyes followed the road. "Dangerous Curve. High Accident Zone." She read the words of the warning sign as they passed it. She didn't notice that Macko was struggling to stay awake. She couldn't contain her excitement and relief. Her man was going to be well again. He would once again be the Macko she knew. She leant over and kissed him, leaving her shining colourless lipstick on his cheek. Macko shot her a quick smile. Rose enjoyed watching Macko drive. It was something he did really well. She leaned over again, found Macko's cheek, puckering her lips into a long kissing sound that stretched out after the kiss.

"Babe, we are on the dangerous road." Macko was smiling despite himself. He was also enjoying the drive. He loved to see Rose's happiness, and enjoyed the affection that came with it. He laughed. "You, babe!" He shook his head with a smile.

Rose giggled too: "You know, my man, when you

are laughing I feel some chocolate cake in my veins. Damn, I love it when you laugh!"

Macko laughed again, and they both laughed together. Rose gave him another kiss, and Macko opened his mouth. Rose shut his lips with her fourth finger. "I know what you are going to say," she said.

"And that is…?"

"Babe, we are on the dangerous road." Rose imitated Macko's deep voice. They both laughed for longer this time, unable to stop them themselves.

"Oh, now you are reading my mind?" Macko said with a smile.

Rose threw up her hands. "Why not? You are my man! Who else should read your mind? And I have a right to kiss you whenever I like, wherever I like."

"I agree with you, babe. You know what?" Macko said as he navigated a sharp curve on the road.

"What, babe?" Rose asked, looking over at him, raising her legs and wriggling in her seat.

"Kiss me again!" Macko shouted.

"Yippp!" She kissed him, not on the cheek this time, but on the mouth.

"Hmmm, thanks, babe. I am glad you are wearing a colourless lipstick. Imagine if it was your favourite one."

She lifted her handbag, pretended to beat Macko with it. "Which one is my favourite?"

"The maroon one, like the dress you are wearing. I love this dress, it reminds me of our special moment. Our first date."

"Yes, babe, I love maroon. I didn't think you would notice things like the colours I choose." She leaned into Macko again and kissed him on the cheek. She counted her kisses. "One!" She gave him the first. "Two!" The second one lasted longer. "Three!" She kissed him for the third time, and then leant back satisfied.

Macko remembered Rose on their first date, in a maroon dress, then pushed the image out of his mind. He concentrated on driving. Rose kissed him again. By now, his cheek was shining with the glow of Rose's lipstick. His skin was always dry, grey-tinged – even when he used lotion. Even Vaseline, even baby oil.

The road ahead narrowed to two lanes – their lane and the oncoming traffic lane. Macko followed the road with his eyes. Beside him, Rose was silent, staring out the window. His eyes closed and he forced them open. Followed the road. H is lids dropped again and the taxi slid across into the oncoming lane. Macko didn't notice. He didn't see the other car, a silver Porsche, appear out of nowhere, travelling at high speed. Its hooter filled the silence, its brights flicked as it crossed to the left-hand side, driving in the yellow lane.

Macko's eyes popped. Instinctively, he hit the brakes. Rose sat frozen in surprise. Everything happened very quickly. She saw the face of the young white man driving the silver Porsche. His face was twisted, his mouth open in a scream. His window was down and she caught a fragment, "Fucking taxi drivers!" She saw his hand fly out the car window, form a fist, and raise a middle finger.

Shaken, Macko looked at Rose. "You must bear in mind that the owner of this taxi will crash us if we crash his taxi."

"Ag, that one!" Rose waved her hand.

"And I still wonder why he lent me this taxi to come so far. Sometimes you could swear that someone is controlling his moods."

"Don't think too much," Rose said. "You are his

employee, he should take care of you."

Macko wiped his eyes with his left hand while steering with the right. His eyes saw eight lanes even though his mind knew there were only two. He thought he could hear the "kiri kiri kiri" sound somewhere. "I'm sleepy or dizzy. I don't know what is happening." Macko stretched his neck.

"Don't stress." Rose touched Macko's shoulder.

"Is there any cooldrink left?" he asked.

"No, not even water. We should stop and buy something at the next garage we pass." Rose kissed Macko on the cheek. "Calm down, babe."

Macko glanced at Rose and winked. She winked back and moved her fingers along his neck.

"I'm feeling better now, I just need to rest, and then we have only two hours left to home." Macko sat straighter and shifted gear.

Rose said, "I love when you are strong and healthy." She pointed. "Look! At last there is a sign for a garage coming up."

She took out her cellphone to take a picture of the eye-catching sunset light in the sky – a light that rose like a hand thrust upward.

Macko jumped. He saw a moving person's shadow on the back seat in the rearview mirror. "What's that?" he asked.

"It's a beautiful light, babe. You see?" Rose said.

Macko checked the mirror before answering Rose. There was no shadow any more. He pretended to be talking about the light outside. "Yes, very beautiful. But not more beautiful than you."

Rose smiled. Night was approaching fast now, and the eye-capturing light was draining away fast. "Ah, it's gone now. And I wonder why it does not appear on my camera. This phone took the picture very well,

I saw." She kept peering at her cellphone, pressing buttons. There was no picture of the hand-like light.

Macko was holding his neck again. Rose noticed, but did not say anything.

Finally, one hour away from home, they saw the garage. Macko pulled off the road and parked the taxi next to the single petrol pump. An old one, brown and rusted. It didn't look like it was working. Macko shone his lights on it, and hit the hooter. No one came to help them. Next to a big tree was a shop with a sign on the door: "Open." Macko hit the hooter again. Still no one came to help.

"Babe, I don't trust this place." Rose shivered.

Macko looked Rose directly in the eyes. "I am here to protect you. Don't worry. Feel safe." He opened the taxi door and got out. Rose jumped a little when he shut the door. With him gone, the taxi felt too big. She wished she had gone with him.

"Hello! Hello!" Macko shouted. "Anybody here to help us?" Nothing, except a wind that kept stirring the leaves of the big tree. The leaves didn't fall. They just kept flying in the wind. To where?

Macko looked back at the taxi, hesitating. Rose was waving her hand, calling him back to the taxi. He saw her waving hand, but it appeared to tell him to go into the shop. He turned back to the shop and noticed a line of drops going from the pump to the shop door. Macko scuffed at the drops with his shoe, and they spread.

He knocked at the shop door. "Hello! Hello!" he called again. "Is this a place for a human being? Hello! Hello! I am asking?" He opened the door cautiously. "Hello? Hello?" There was no answer, but he heard voices. He entered, but there was no sign of anyone. "Hello! Hello!" No one answered him.

He saw a rusted fridge filled with rusted cans of cooldrink. There was a wooden counter next to it. He looked up. Above him hung shards of glass of different colours, linked together by what looked like a spider's web. They hit against each other, making a sharp noise that shot up Macko's spine into his head. He held his ears closed. The wind kept the fragments of glass moving, clinking. The wind howled outside. The door he had entered began to close slowly. His joints became weak. He saw a shadow, a movement. His heart started to race. No, it was just a cat. It threaded itself around his legs, making strange mewling sounds. Suddenly an old man rose up from behind the counter. Macko stood still, staring. The man had uncombed grey hair and a smile that revealed sharp dirty teeth. "Can I help you? This is the way home!" said the old man.

Macko felt his scalp crawl. He backed away, then ran for the door. As he reached it, it slammed shut. He grabbed the handle, rattled and shook it, leaned against it with his full weight. It gave way and he ran to the taxi, not looking back.

He climbed in, panting. Rose looked at his empty hands.

"This is a haunted garage," Macko said as he fed the key into the ignition.

"That is what I thought. That was why I was calling you," Rose was shaking.

"You called me? Were you not telling me to go inside?" Macko asked.

"No, babe. Let's get out of this place, please!" Rose's voice was pitched high.

Macko started the engine. Felt a flood of relief as he heard the motor roar. They returned to the main road. It was almost empty, only a few trucks, easily passed. Macko put his foot down. The road was clear. He took advantage of it. And there were no cameras. They passed several long trucks. There were no curves any more. The road was straight. The taxi's right headlight went dim, then died. Macko didn't mind. They were near their town. Only twenty minutes left.

When Macko blinked, he saw the shiny eyes of an animal. He heard the bang. They'd hit it. The taxi swerved off the road, Macko fighting to gain control. Too late. They found themselves in the dirt next to a field of sunflowers. They got out of the taxi. There was blood on the bonnet and the windscreen was badly cracked. They walked slowly back up to the road to see what kind of animal they had hit. They couldn't find a body. Macko walked up and down while Rose watched. "It must have been a donkey or a cow. Did you see the windshield? Did you see what it did?" Macko kept walking, looking. Eventually Rose called him back. She was tired. They climbed down off the road, following the trail cut by the taxi's wheels, and got back in. Macko turned the key several times, and finally the engine took. Back on the road, he used the taxi's remaining headlight to look for the dead animal in the bushes. They looked and looked. There was nothing.

"Today is the worst day of all!" Macko said, as he turned the taxi towards their town.

"I know, babe. But look on the other side. The trusted doctor of Jagersfontein confirmed that you can get well again." Rose said, looking at Macko. "It was worth it, babe."

Macko was silent. The lights of Qwaqwa were before them. They arrived at their place.

Thirteen

"HERE WE ARE!" Macko stretched his hands up. He yawned, then turned his head and smiled at the passengers. Some smiled back at him, others not. One of the passengers, sitting near the passenger door, leaned over and opened it. The wind swept into the taxi. Qwaqwa was wrapped in a dense mist, hovering around the mountains. In Qwaqwa, the winters were harsh. The occupants of Macko's taxi braced themselves against the cold, a cold that pierced through the bones to the marrow. It was the time of the year when even dogs had to find a hiding place to stay warm.

Most of the commuters were already on their cellphones, notifying their loved ones that they had arrived. Some were new to the town and needed help – where to from here?

"Where are the local taxis?" asked a young man, his eyes directed through the window, trying to get his bearings.

"There are no taxis at this time. It is late," Macko responded.

The man stared at Macko as if he didn't understand the words.

"Where are you going?" Macko asked.

"They said I should get off next to the information centre," he said.

Macko noticed that the youngster's eyes were red, and he kept pressing his nose with his fingers. He sneezed and sneezed.

"But we passed the information centre. Why didn't you ask in time?" Macko was irritated. "You might be lucky and get some taxi to take you from there."

"Okay, thanks." The young man got out slowly. His luggage was heavy: a big suitcase and a transparent plastic bag containing a blanket. He looked like a student. Yes, the universities were opening for the second semester. Students rested in June. Now it was their time again. Macko guessed he must be a new student, one registering for the first time in the second semester. The young man picked up his bag and began walking, then dropped it again and stood looking lost.

"Bro Macko…!"

Macko looked around to see who was calling him. He flicked on his lights. The beams lit up a figure moving towards him. It was too dark to make out any features; all he saw was the black shape of a man coming towards him. The lights at the rank had been broken since summer. It hadn't been so bad then, but now that it was winter, the sun set early and the dark covered the rank like a blanket, making it difficult to see anything. Macko recognised Dodo only at the last minute.

"You'll drop me at Mojalefa's corner, right?" Dodo laughed at Macko's surprised face.

Macko shook his head. He closed his window. He climbed out and assisted the commuters removing the big bags stored in the back. In no time Dodo was next to him, helping him.

"I am looking for a taxi that is going to Tsheseng,"

said a young woman. She was holding a child's hand and carried an infant on her back.

Before Macko could say anything, Dodo answered, "There are no taxis to the village at this time of the day, my sister."

The young woman with her children looked steadily at them. "So what should I do? How to get to the village?"

"Next to that garage. You see it?" Macko pointed. "Pass that corner and you'll get the meter taxi there, they will take you home with a special fee."

"Okay, thanks, driver." She lifted the suitcase Macko had just unloaded and walked away, heaving the case in one hand, the other clutching the child.

"What about us who don't have money for the meter taxis?" asked one of the passengers, standing next to the unloaded luggage.

Macko was about to reply when his phone rang. He stepped aside to check who the call was from, then answered it with a smile.

Dodo glanced over at Macko, seeing the smile, and looked back at the passenger. "It is not the driver's problem any more. You have to sort yourself out. You don't have a car, that's why you are using public transport. So this is public transport, not your own transport."

None of the remaining passengers said anything after that. They hefted their bags and began to walk away. Macko hung up, smiling and blushing a little after the phone conversation. He moved back to his taxi. The rank was emptying. Those who had money went to find the meter taxis. Others waited for loved ones to arrive to pick them up. Those who had no money or loved ones were on their own.

Macko and Dodo were also about to leave when

the silence that had descended on the rank was broken. Screams pierced the darkness. They made the hair on Macko's neck prickle. A man's voice. The words were distinct. It was a call for help. Macko and Dodo exchanged looks and set off at the same time, running towards the nearby road, where the sound seemed to come from. As they approached, they saw the shapes of three men running away. They were wearing hats pulled low over their eyes, making it impossible to see their features. Further along, they saw a young man standing with his suitcase lid popped open and his possessions scattered across the pavement. Macko recognised the young man as the student he had directed to the information centre. Seeing the young man's tear-stained face, his empty hands, and the suitcase, Macko immediately knew what had happened. The men who had run away must have been robbing him. His and Dodo's approach had probably scared them off.

"Eish, little brother. I am sorry." Macko bent to help him gather his things and pack them back into the suitcase. When they were done, he held the young man's shoulder. "Come with us, we will leave you at the police station so that you can report the matter."

The young man nodded. Tears were still streaming down his cheeks.

"Here you must be very careful, grootman," Dodo said.

Macko picked up the suitcase, and the three of them walked to the taxi in silence.

A few passengers were still lingering, clutching their belongings. The incident had put them on edge.

"If I had enough petrol, I would take you all to your different homes," Macko told them. He started the taxi. Macko, Dodo, and the young man drove away from the rank, leaving the remaining passengers stranded. The young man was still crying, wiping his tears from time to time. Macko's cellphone sounded. It was an SMS: "My lion, please fly to me. I miss you dearly." Macko grinned.

"What is going on? Is someone in love?" Dodo asked. Macko blushed. Soon they were at the police station. Macko went inside with the young man, leaving Dodo in the taxi.

Inside, a loud noise welcomed them. A drunken couple at the front desk were reporting each other, each demanding the other's arrest. Shouting at each other. Insulting each other. Two police officers emerged from a passage and helped the desk officer throw them out. They were still shouting as they disappeared out the door. Macko laughed to himself, thinking of the fights he and Rose sometimes had. The young man glanced at him, and Macko fell silent again. A lady with many documents she needed to certify was now at the desk.

Macko and the young man sat down, waiting to be helped. They watched as the reception area filled with police officers. Several of them were carrying long rifles. It seemed like something was going down. The officers slipped on bulletproof vests as they headed to the door. Macko overheard bits of their conversation: "There are thugs in the ranks. They just robbed and raped some young lady who arrived from Johannesburg. Can you believe it, they did this in front of her toddler and young infant."

Macko felt his back tense. He was so distracted by what he had heard, he didn't notice Baile's arrival. Macko looked up and froze. He recognised the man's rusted teeth. Then he shook himself right and jumped to his feet. His eyes clashed with the detective's eyes, which seemed to have no irises, forming dark pools. He shivered, and his voice shook slightly. "Hello Detective, they just robbed this young man at the rank."

Baile didn't say anything. He turned and waved his hand for them to go with him. The young man stood and followed. Macko sighed, then followed them as well – what choice did he have? As they kept moving along a long corridor, paint peeling from the walls, it seemed to grow narrow and the floor seemed to slope. Macko felt like he was suffocating in the stale air.

"Where are we going?" he asked. The words echoed back at him, louder with each reverberation, and he covered his ears. His brow was sweating and his feet suddenly felt very heavy, as if he was sinking. He called "Wait!", trying to get the detective's attention, but Baile didn't answer. His head was no longer visible. He was just a long coat moving on black shoes. Macko pulled his eyes from the detective to the young man, and recoiled in horror. The young man's head was also gone. His black-and-white shirt travelled on bare feet. Macko started to turn, but now the walls started to crack. Next to him, the young man's shape paused, turned to Macko. It waved its bodiless hand, telling Macko to follow. Macko turned and ran like a headless chicken, never looking back. The light bulbs hanging from the roof were shaking as he ran. Sweat washed his body. In front of him, a dark entrance loomed, and he felt his breath leaving his body. He was about to collapse when he burst back into the front room in which they had met the detective.

Macko stood breathing heavily. The police officers at the desk looked at him in surprise. He collected himself. His hands were shaking as he crossed to a small water dispenser. He lifted one of the disposable white cups and filled it. He took a quick sip, trying to control the shaking.

"My broer, what took you so long?" Dodo asked. "Your phone has been ringing. I picked it up for you."

Macko finished the water in a long gulp before he answered Dodo. "Who was it?" He was blinking non-stop. He didn't want to look at Dodo. He didn't want him to realise how terrified he had been.

"Jou vrou! I told her you are helping some seun. She said she is very proud of you." Dodo smiled. "What did you feed her? I've never heard jou vrou so happy."

Macko felt the tension start to leave his body. He smiled a little, then became serious again. "Let's just say we had a wonderful trip last week. It changed everything. She is in love with me like she never was before."

"Jesus! I wish I was you," whistled Dodo. "Ja, I noticed you were not around. Jim was driving that scrap taxi of yours. Now look, Mr Tabola has given you a new taxi. Good things are happening for you, my broer. I am happy for you."

"That scrap gave me a tough time, but I miss it. It was my best babe," Macko said.

"Why are we turning here now? Authi ya ka, nna ke ya ha ka – my dear brother, I am going to my home. My vrou is waiting for me, I need a sparkling relationship like you. You know these women!"

"We are just quickly going to buy electricity at the shopping centre before they close." Macko increased the volume of the CD player and balanced the powerful speakers. The bass was loud. Their taxi roared like a happy lion. Inside, there were sparkling lights along the roof. Changing colours: from blue to green, from yellow to red. The leather seats made it more splendid, more comfortable.

When they arrived at the local shopping centre, they attracted attention. The bass of a house song –

"Shumaya" by DBN Nyts, featuring Zinhle Ngidi – boomed from the speakers and filled the parking area. People gathered, and even the old ones moved their bodies. Macko and Dodo left the taxi windows open and went to stand in the queue for electricity. The lights inside the taxi kept sparkling.

The queue was not that long. There were only ten people in front of them.

"Our municipality is not fair. We buy this expensive electricity, in no time the load-shedding will visit us," Dodo said, moving his head in time to the song playing from their taxi.

"Don't blame the municipality. This thing is happening all over Mzansi. But we should stop complaining. There are worse countries out there, ask me," said Macko. Everyone turned to listen to them.

"Yes, you are right. But let's not protect Mzansi by saying other countries are worse. The governing political organisation is responsible!" Dodo jived. He went down a little, bending his knees, and up again.

"You won't understand as long you've never lived in or visited other countries. It is really tough out there." Macko took out his money. "Ke kopa motlakase wa hundred." He put the note and the electricity slip through the small window. They listened to the song as it repeated itself. It was getting colder and colder in the queue. People pulled their jackets around them. Almost everyone wore gloves, warm hats, warm boots.

Macko's cellphone rang again, and he answered it. "Hello babe, I'm just buying electricity now."

"Okay, my babe, please hurry! I miss you. I'm gonna grab you..." Rose's voice was audible.

Macko interrupted her with shyness: "Uhm, yes, babe. I am with other people here."

"Okay babe, come home. Please ... love youuuuu!" She hung up.

Macko smiled. He and Dodo returned to the taxi and drove off. In less than ten minutes, he dropped Dodo off at his rusty shack. He decreased the volume of the music and calculated the money of the day.

His puppy was waiting outside when he reached home, wagging its tail, happy to see him. It greeted the taxi with a bark. Macko parked and took out the money. He locked all the doors, and made sure that all the windows were closed. He was more careful now than he had been with his beloved scrap. He played with his puppy, lifting his hands up and down. It jumped and jumped and barked happily. He thought of letting it in the house, but he didn't want to destroy Rose's sweet mood. He entered, closing the door gently behind him.

"Honey, I'm home."

The house was very warm. It was clean and tidy. The smell of the floor polish made Macko smile. The smell of food made him hungry. Rose welcomed him with a long, soft kiss. She hugged and hugged him.

"Love, I am proud of you. I'm really glad that you are healed now. The psychologist really helped," Rose kissed him again and smiled. She wore a new nightgown and a sexy smile. She pulled him into the dining room. Music was playing. Not just any music, but real music: "One Man Woman" by Milira Jones, followed by "No More Tears" by Anita Baker.

Rose had lit candles and their soft light filled the room. There were dishes filled with food on the table. She opened a bottle of red wine and poured for them. Blushing, Macko lifted his glass, and touched it against her glass. They smiled at each other. Rose opened the lid of one of the dishes and took out a ripe strawberry.

She dipped it in cream, and lifted it to Macko's mouth. He bit one half. The juice filled his mouth. Rose laughed and ate the other half. They kissed a little, tasting the strawberry in each other's mouths. Rose pulled away and stood to dish the main meal. It was oxtail with homemade dumplings, Macko's favourite. He melted. He smiled. He chuckled. Rose gave him a warm cloth to clean his hands. He ate and ate. He wanted more of the oxtail, but Rose shook her head with a smile. She dished out dessert. Homemade smooth custard, with a red raspberry jelly, sliced white peaches with malva pudding, strawberries and cream on the side. They ate to the sweet sounds of "Beautiful In My Eyes" by Joshua Kadison, followed by "Hold Me In Your Arms" by Teddy Pendergrass.

Afterwards, Rose took all the dishes to the kitchen and left them in the washing bowl. She returned from the kitchen and blew out the candles. She took Macko's hand, and led him towards the bedroom. The bedding was fresh, the sheets new. The sounds of Freddie Jackson's "Rock Me Tonight" accompanied them. Rose opened her new nightgown and Macko leaned in and kissed each breast, his lips soft against her nipples. Rose closed her eyes, opened them. Her gown slid off and her shaved perfumed pussy smiled at Macko. He ran his lips down her body. Breasts. Ribs. Belly button. Waist. Abdomen. Kissed her vagina. Held its lips with his mouth's lips. He put his tongue in, enjoying the taste. Hmmmm. Rose moaned as she closed her eyes and spread her legs, kicking off her slippers and standing with one leg on the bed.

Macko stood up, and Rose undressed him, sliding his boxer shorts off slowly.

They fell onto the bed, Rose on top of Macko. She rubbed herself against Macko's hard machine. "Ahhh, babe, it is coming! Yes, yes, yes!" Rose screamed. Her vibrations swept through Macko's body and she collapsed on his chest. They flipped, with Macko now on top. Then a switch tripped in his head. Rose's moans sounded like the cries of children. He tried to block them out, but the voices wouldn't leave him. Every time Rose opened her mouth, he heard a small, desperate, piercing cry. No, not now, not now. He tried to ignore the cries. He focused on Rose. Her body. Her tits. Her pussy. The cries grew louder. Rose didn't notice anything wrong until Macko's penis died inside her.

She opened her eyes to find Macko clutching his head. "Oh babe! Are you okay? Let me find your medication!" She jumped up and ran to the kitchen, poured a glass of water, and retrieved his pills.

She found Macko looking ashamed and puzzled.

"What happened?" Macko asked.

"It's you, babe. You freaked me out. I am glad you are okay." She got back into bed. "Let us sleep. You gave me rough, marvellous sex. But it is not enough: you owe me."

They laughed. They cuddled, then slept.

Fourteen

It was quarter to eleven. Macko was close to his taxi, smoking a rare cigarette, watching Dodo. Dodo kept himself busy by washing taxis. Taxi drivers would pay him even when they hadn't asked him to wash their vehicles. That was how it worked. He would do the job, and they would pay, albeit often grudgingly. That was how he was able to bring something home to eat. He was busy washing a blue twenty-one seater Sprinter. He loved his work. All the Sprinter's mats were out. He soaked and rinsed them. The blue body was shining. Now he was polishing the tyres, bending his body. Half his arse was out of his trousers, which were slowly slipping down. Even if he noticed, he didn't mind. He was working and happy.

Two young women approached. He didn't hear them coming. They looked at Dodo's exposed bum. One pointed with a naughty smile. The other one grabbed her friend's pointing hand. She was also smiling, but she shook her head in rebuke. Dodo was busy, dipping an old brush into a tin of polish.

"Hello bhuti," the two young women greeted simultaneously. They held their bags in their hands. One dragged an orange wheeled suitcase. She was wearing black jeans and an orange pullover that showed her cleavage. The other one carried a pink bag with a white Nike sign on it, slung on her shoulder. The lipstick on her mouth was also pink. So was her tracksuit. Even her white takkies had pink stripes. She was paler than her friend.

Dodo cleared his throat. He dropped his black polish container and brush and wiped his hands on his trousers. He drew himself erect, pulled up his trousers and smiled at the ladies.

"Hello, beautiful sisters," he greeted them.

"Re kopa ho botsa – may we please ask," said the one in the orange pullover, mixing Sesotho with English with an isiZulu accent, not aware she was repeating herself.

"Where is a Johannesburg taxi?" the other one asked.

Dodo took time to answer. He was looking at the cleavage of the young woman in the orange pullover. He put his hand over his mouth, coughed, and said, "Have you registered your names and paid at that cashier's window?"

They looked at each other and said, "No."

"Okay. Let me help you with your bags." He lifted the bag and the suitcase. You could see that they were heavy. Poor Dodo. "You'll find me at that taxi," he gestured at Macko's taxi with his head. "Go and pay."

The young women went to the cashier's window and Dodo went to Macko's taxi. He dropped the bags, panting. He didn't even greet his friend; he snatched the water bottle from his hands and gulped the contents without stopping. Five hundred millilitres gone.

Macko laughed at him. "I've been watching you. Will you wash and polish my taxi, or I am going to show your wife this video I just took on my cellphone?"

"Ag, it's just a video. Go and show her," Dodo said. He saw the two young women approaching and checked his appearance in the taxi's mirror. Taking out his cellphone, he asked, "May I please have your digits?"

The women looked at each other. The one with pink lipstick said, "Don't you dare take advantage of us!"

"Which advantage now?" Disappointed, Dodo put his phone back in his pocket.

Macko laughed. He held up his phone and continued to video Dodo.

"Bhuti, is this a taxi to Johannesburg?" The young woman with pink lipstick looked at Macko.

"Yes," Macko answered. He stopped filming, and the girls opened the passenger door. Macko and Dodo watched their long legs slide inside, feet disappearing. Dodo shrugged, then went back to his work, leaving their bags outside the taxi.

It was half-past twelve. An old man arrived. He was not pleased to see that he was only number three. He climbed in slowly and sat down.

"Sir, have you registered?" one of the young women asked.

"Yes, my child. I am in the correct taxi, right? To Egoli, Johannesburg?" he asked.

The young woman with the pink lipstick laughed and her friend answered, "Yebo, baba."

All around them taxis were filling up, departing for their different destinations. People came, but they kept passing Macko's taxi, to the disappointment of the young women and the old man. The clock was ticking.

"Apples! Apples!" the fruitseller shouted. "My lovely customers. Red apples! Green apples! Gold apples! They are all sweet!" She shouted after those who were not buying. If a taxi door was open, she stood at it and shouted. If the door was closed, she shouted at the windows.

"Is this a taxi to Johannes…?" a young man asked.

One of the young women interrupted him before he could finish getting the word out of his mouth. "Yes, yes, my brother. Get in."

He greeted and got in. The old man and young women greeted him back.

One o'clock arrived.

"Remote batteries. Watch batteries. Radio batteries!" The seller was a man wearing a brown two-piece from Dickies. A brown woollen hat. Dark-brown All Stars. His mouth was blacker than coal. He had three scars: one on the nose, another one under the right eye, and the last one on the forehead. No one bought from him, and he went to another taxi.

Cold air began to remind everyone that it was winter. It was half-past one. The young women whispered a little, then stood up.

"Sir," they said to the old man. He didn't hear. He was sleeping. They looked at the young man. He stared up in confusion. Saw their mouths move, took one headphone off his left ear.

"Our brother, we are coming back. We are hungry. We have been here for some time now." They got out. The young man nodded. He put his headphones back.

Two o'clock arrived. Three people came, a family: a father, his wife, and their toddler. They got in. After a while, the two young women returned, carrying KFC. They were a little happier to see another three people. A hobo followed them. They got into the taxi and quickly closed the door.

The hobo went to a window: "My sister, please. Just a piece of KFC," he asked, holding his stomach.

They kept quiet. He stood there, staring at them eating.

"Even a bone is okay. Please," he continued to ask.

"He says even a bone," said the old man, now awake.

"No, just look at him. He is very healthy. Why doesn't he go and look for work?" the young woman asked, food in her mouth.

"What did you say, my child?" asked the old man.

"Just look at him. He knows how to ask for money. Why doesn't he ask for a job instead?" She shook her head and continued to eat.

"They live here, this is how they make a living. They even sleep here," the old man said.

"Whatever, we work hard, and they just wake up to beg from us?" She waved her oily hand. People laughed. After a while, the poor hobo gave up and went off. It was half-past three when a smartly dressed lady arrived, wearing a blue leather skirt with a matching top. The gold watch on her wrist shone together with the ring on her left second finger.

"I really think they should mix us. It is getting late," the old man said.

"Yes, you are right," the woman in blue agreed.

The old man stretched his neck, "Where is that driver? We should tell him."

"I don't know where he is. I saw him when we arrived here around twelve o'clock," one of the young women said, also craning and looking around.

"A warm, fresh mielie, dear visitors. A warm mielie to keep you warm," called a young lady outside the taxi. She opened the door. People felt the cold air coming from the outside. "A fresh mielie!"

"Is it really fresh?" the woman in blue leather asked.

"Yes, it is really fresh, madam," she answered.

"How much is it?"

"Only fifteen rand for you, madam." She lifted a mielie out of her tin.

The woman took out her purse and gave her a twenty-rand note. The seller gave her a warm mielie and her change.

"Thank you, madam. Lovely passengers, are you sure you don't want a warm mielie?" she asked again. No one answered. She was about to close the passenger door when a guy wearing a green security uniform got in.

"My phone is flat. Why don't they mix us with the Pretoria and Vereeniging passengers?" said the lady in the orange pullover, glancing at her cellphone.

"Yes, it is now four o'clock. Let us all go and ask for our money back if they don't mix us." The young woman with pink lipstick stood up. "Let us go, it is getting late!"

"I wonder if I am still going. We are going to arrive in Johannesburg around nine o'clock, and I have to take another taxi to Carletonville. And I won't find any taxi to Carletonville at that time. Thugs will just rob us if we arrive there at that time. Last week they robbed my sick friend. They really don't have any mercy," complained the old man. "I just want my money back. I will wake early tomorrow morning and go to Johannesburg then."

The toddler cried, and the mother scooped up her child and put her on her back.

"But taking back your money will just decrease our number. Okay, good people, let us go to demand that they mix us, or demand our money back," said the young woman with pink lipstick as she got out of the taxi.

"I have to go to work tonight, otherwise they are going to deduct from my wages. I really can't afford that," complained the guy in the security uniform.

The woman in blue also stood, still eating her mielie,

and said, "I am going to an interview tomorrow. This taxi must go!"

They got out and went to the cashier's office, led by the lady with the pink lipstick. The cashier directed them to Tabola's office.

The mighty Tabola was in his office with his secretary. Hearing the voices outside, he took out his gun.

"Calm down, boss," said the secretary. "There is no need for a weapon. It is easy to solve this situation." He left Tabola in the office and went outside. "Dear passengers, what is wrong?"

"It is getting late. We just want to be mixed so that we can arrive before it is too late and dark in Johannesburg. That is all," said the pink lipstick lady.

"I want my money back. I can't and won't risk going at this time," the old man said.

The secretary clapped his hands once, and said, "Well, I hear you all. May you kindly go to your taxi now, I am coming. Those who want their money back will get it at five o'clock exactly."

Without saying anything, the passengers returned to the taxi. Along the way, they encountered Macko, heading in the opposite direction. It was fifteen minutes past four.

Macko arrived at the office, passing the secretary, who was puffing a smoke outside.

"Exactly what is your problem?" Macko demanded, entering Tabola's office. He stood in front of his boss's desk and pointed his finger.

"What the hell are you talking about now?" Tabola left the cards he was playing and stood up.

"Number one, seven people died last week because of the taxi violence! Number two, if you and your associates had allowed the Gauteng taxi that was here earlier to take the passengers to Johannesburg while I took your taxi to the mechanic, those passengers would be home by now," Macko shouted.

"You are just a driver. Stop involving yourself..." Tabola held his hand at his waist, next to his gun.

"I know you are behind this taxi violence. Are you not satisfied with the number of people you killed so far?" Saliva flew out of Macko's angry mouth and washed Tabola's face.

"Get out! I say, out!" Tabola put his hand on his gun. "You want to put your life at risk? Remember, you don't belong in South Africa. Remember, I have access to that bitch of yours."

"What do you mean by 'access'?"

"Just get out of my way. You are only a driver, I pay you to drive. Now go and drive. Take these people to Johannesburg."

Macko stormed out of the office. He met the secretary and grabbed the man, held him, one hand on his chest. "How do you let this person kill people?"

The secretary was about to speak, but then they heard Tabola on the phone. "This is our territory. Let us kill those who are in our way. Let us clean out those Gauteng cockroaches. Shoot to kill. Shoot!"

Macko didn't wait for the secretary's answer. He ran back to his taxi. He stumbled over Dodo's washing bucket and water flew. The handle broke. The cashier was in the taxi, counting the number of passengers and refunding the old man. It was exactly five o'clock.

Although Macko was enraged, he was ready to drive. But now something else stopped him. The taxi keys were nowhere to be found. He searched his pockets. There were no keys. He searched his taxi. There were no keys. He looked under the seats. There were no keys. He looked on the ground next to the taxi. There were no keys. He pulled himself upright and returned to Tabola's office. He searched the floor while Tabola sat and laughed at him.

"It is the third time this driver has lost his taxi keys. I wonder who has bewitched him?" said an old woman who had a fruit stall, clapping her hands several times. "That driver who said 'the taxi industry is built up on the blood of innocent people' was correct – phhhh!" she spat on the floor and warmed her hands on the fire she had made in an iron bucket pierced with holes.

The few people left at the rank were all angry. "Taxis! They will always be like this. Fuck the taxi industry!" Insults flew. "These dirty dogs are very selfish!"

Tabola had meanwhile summoned Jim to go and look for the last set of spare keys for Macko's taxi at his home. In no time, Jim returned with the keys. He gave them to Tabola, who held them in the air and told Macko to come and get them.

Macko grabbed the keys, held them and squeezed until the sharp metal pierced his skin. He did not say thank you. He walked to his taxi with his head down. There was blood on the keys. His palm burned as he clasped the steering wheel. He slipped the bloody key in the ignition. The engine roared. He pumped the gas so it roared again. Quarter to six. It was dark. The taxi exited the rank.

Fifteen

YOU COULD HEAR the engine of Tabola's black 4X4 coming: Isuzu diesel. He arrived at the rank and stopped. The taxis ahead of him weren't moving. Many engines were still running, but the driver's seats were all empty. Tabola hit his hooter. He stretched his neck, trying to see what was holding up the traffic, but taxis blocked his view. "You could swear that these drivers are of the same mother!"

He turned his engine off, climbed out his 4X4 and slammed the door. "What the hell is going on here?" He strode forward, his grey leather sandals kicking up dust. No one answered him. He passed six taxis. On the corner, he collided with a boy handing out pamphlets. The pamphlets flew up into the air, then scattered on the ground: "Great Herbalist from Northern Africa, Dr Moyo. Bring back your lost lover! Win lotto and casino! Cleansing for good luck! Penis enlargement! Unwanted discharge!" Tabola kicked the pamphlets and continued on his way.

The boy ran after him: "Hey! Look what you did!"

Tabola didn't bother to look back.

The boy shrugged. "Anyway, you helped me to reduce them. They were many," he smiled to himself as he bent to collect the undamaged ones off the ground.

Another boy came running up to him. His

pamphlets advertised "Dr Otongo! Powerful Herbalist from Mali! Quick, safe abortion! Win court cases! Get a good job! Attract someone you love! Strong erection! Recover your stolen goods! Magic stick! If you want a man to pay you lobola!" He looked at his colleague crawling around on the ground, retrieving his pamphlets. "Who did this? He must pay you!"

The boy on the ground raised his head: "What would you do if bro Tabola did this to you?"

The other boy whistled and shook his head. He left his friend on the ground, and went back to his work, flicking his wrist and snapping a pamphlet at a passing couple.

Tabola passed the stalls of the mothers selling food and another six parked taxis. Finally he found the driver responsible for disrupting the rank's traffic. A young man with a full load had stopped to argue with the other drivers who were waiting for their taxis to fill up. The argument was about yesterday's soccer match, the Soweto derby: Pirates versus Chiefs.

"It was a penalty!" he shouted as his taxi idled behind him.

Tabola went straight to the taxi, stretched his hands to the keys and turned off the engine. He approached the driver, who was too engrossed in his argument to notice.

"It is true, gents, we were supposed to win that game!"

A few of the drivers laughed, then fell silent when they saw Tabola appear behind him.

"What is wrong now, gents?"

Tabola klapped the young driver on the head with his meaty hand.

"Fuck you! Who the hell are you?" the driver said as he swung around, raising his hands to klap back whoever had klapped him. He saw Tabola and slowly lowered his hands.

Tabola pointed to his taxi blocking the traffic. "You think this is your mother's rank!" He hit him again in the face, on the forehead. As the driver turned to run to his taxi, Tabola kicked him on the backside. The driver speeded up, swung the door of his taxi open, started the engine, and flew out of the rank.

"What are you looking at? Get back to work!" Tabola shouted.

Taxi drivers whistled as Tabola passed. Macko, who had watched the whole incident, shook his head. He was not impressed. He started towards Tabola, but Dodo stopped him. Tabola didn't notice. He went to his 4X4. Traffic was starting to clear. As he drove past, Macko spat on the ground, but Tabola didn't see. His mind was on important business.

He parked in his reserved spot next to the office, unlocked it and put his keys on the desk. He took out his cellphone. Scrolled, looking for a number. He picked up the office phone and dialled.

Rose was chopping a tomato when her cellphone rang. She looked at it. She didn't answer it. It rang again. She looked at it, and continued to chop and chop. It rang for a third time. She put the knife on the table, licked her fingers, answered.

"Rose, hello!" A rude voice. "Why don't you want to answer my calls?"

"I knew it was your office, but was not sure if it was you," Rose replied. "And why are you calling me from the office phone?"

"Okay, you know MTN to Vodacom during the day is expensive. Now if you were using an MTN number…" Tabola started.

"Oh, okay, but I don't expect that from a man of

your calibre. Does that mean I'm not worthy to be called by your cellphone because I'm using MTN?" Rose continued to chop. She had her cellphone pressed between her ear and shoulder.

"Don't fight with me. I am bored, that's why I called you," Tabola lowered his voice.

"Oh, and where is your principal?"

"She is a principal at Tlhorong School, not my principal. The schools are closed, so she took a vacation to her parents' home with my kids. It is eight days now. I miss you. I am hungry," Tabola said.

"Oh, you miss me only when you are bored? Anyway, my man is around, so you know we can't risk it. Goodbye," said Rose.

"I can think of something."

Their conversation was interrupted by a knock on Tabola's office door.

"Please don't hang up." Tabola held the phone away from his face and shouted, "Come in."

"Boss, I just wanted to tell you that I'm off on that special trip. Contract workers finished with their job in Bloemfontein," Jim said, holding his woollen hat in his hands.

"Oh, that special! Are you not tired? Macko will take that special for you, as today's trip to Joburg can't succeed. There are not enough people going to Jozi. And of course you will get your full wage at the end of the week."

"Dankie, boss, plus I have some flu. I will tell Macko on my way out, as they said they were already waiting for the taxi from us."

"Okay. No, don't tell Macko. I will tell him myself, just tell him to come to the office urgently."

Jim left and Tabola returned the phone to his ear. "Hello darling, are you still there?"

"Yes, it is you who told me to wait."

"I just organised something. Macko is about to go to Bloemfontein. Nothing can disturb us now. I will see you in one hour."

There was another knock at the door.

"You don't even ask me, you tell me?" said Rose.

"Please don't be like this. There is someone at the door, I have to go. See you later." He dropped the phone and yelled, "Come in!"

Macko entered. "Boss, Jim said you wanted to see me urgently. Is there any problem?"

"Just a little problem, my dear brother. Jim was supposed to fetch some specials at Bloemfontein. He is not feeling well, besides I trust you for these long trips, as you know. You are my best and most experienced driver. I will add some bucks to this week's wage." Tabola bared his teeth at Macko. "You look surprised, what is it?"

"It is the first time hearing you say I'm your 'dear brother'." Macko looked at Tabola with narrow eyes.

Tabola smiled. "Here are the keys, money for petrol, and the directions. Ke a leboha."

Macko took the money and the paper with directions, and got into his taxi. He took out his cellphone and speed-dialled. "Hello babe, I hope you are well. I am taking an urgent special trip to Bloemfontein. I will be home very late, around eleven at night."

He listened to Rose's understanding reply.

"Mcaaaw … babe. Thank you. I have to go. Byeeee." He hung up the phone and turned the key. The engine roared.

Tabola waited until Macko's taxi left the rank before heading out. He stopped at the shops and bought expensive chocolates and a red transparent panty from Miladys. He sat in his car outside Rose's house, sprayed freshener into his mouth.

He knocked once. Rose was waiting. He dropped the chocolates and the panty on the floor, and kissed her roughly. He unbuttoned her blouse and pushed up her skirt, tearing at her underwear. His belt was open, his boxers and trousers at his feet. He put Rose on the edge of the kitchen table and inserted his hungry penis.

He held her to his body, grasping her breast: "Yes, yes! Oh damn! It is coming!" He moved faster.

Rose responded with a whimper.

He pulled her against him as he released.

"Take it easy, why so rough? I want it nicely. I also want to feel and enjoy it," said Rose taking his hands.

Tabola pulled his hands away. "Let us go to bed."

Macko passed Kestell. He passed Bethlehem. He counted the towns. He was happy when he reached number three, Senekal; he was getting closer to Bloemfontein. Only two towns were left: Paul Roux and Winburg. As he left Senekal, he hit heavy traffic. He strained his head to see the obstruction. Ahead, he could see the accident. A taxi had collided with another taxi, right at the Stop & Go. Shattered heads lolled against windows. Blood painted the glass. Ambulance lights whirled.

Macko pushed himself back in his seat. He drummed his fingers on the wheel. He got out his phone and called Rose. She didn't answer. After thirty minutes, the traffic cleared. He passed a detective directing traffic. The detective put out his hand, approached the taxi, and stuck his head in the window. "You must drive safely! It's dangerous on these roads. You would be better off at home."

Macko hesitated. The detective looked familiar. He ran his words through his head. Looked at the man again, waving for him to drive on. Macko shrugged. He relaxed. Put on Brenda Fassie. He clapped his hands together when the traffic thinned, let the taxi drive itself. But his moment of happiness disappeared as he hit traffic again. Two traffic officers blocked the road. Ahead, maintenance vehicles were still clearing the road. Ambulances were loading bodies. Macko watched their red lights swirl. He was tired. He needed air and a cigarette, but he hadn't brought any. He got out of the taxi. He noticed his Orlando Pirates sticker had fallen off. He stretched his body and walked to the side of the road. Undid his zipper, passed urine. He shook his penis off, buttoned up. Returned to his taxi. Clicked his knuckles. He put on jazz, then changed the disk. He opened the cubbyhole and took out a new sticker that had a green dagga leaf printed on it, with the words "Legalise it".

He took out his cellphone and tried to call Rose again, but there was no network coverage. He sighed and put the phone away. His elbow brushed the hooter as he bent, and he jumped in his seat. The blue lights of police cars kept flickering. The red lights of the ambulances kept flickering. The yellow lights of road-maintenance vehicles flickered, too. Macko pulled his eyes away from the colours. He picked up his cellphone again, scrolled and read through Rose's messages. In no time he was laughing aloud.

"How can someone laugh like this right in the midst of an accident?" Macko heard voices through his window. He turned his head and saw a couple in the car next to him. They were raising their voices so he would be sure to hear. Their words stung. "These useless taxi drivers! They always fail to be patient.

How can that dead driver think of overtaking on the Stop & Go?"

Macko closed his window. He would mind his business, and they should mind theirs.

It took the maintenance vehicles a full hour to finish their work. The officers finally gave the signal and cars started to move again. Macko breathed a sigh of relief as he got back on the road. He had only driven for ten minutes when the phone rang. Macko glanced at the number: one he didn't recognise. He slowed and pulled to the side before answering. Heard static. The network was gone again. He saw the number, but couldn't call back. He tried several times, but failed. Macko decided to get back on the road, but as soon as he turned on the engine, the call came again.

"Hello! Hello! Do you hear me?" a loud voice asked, not waiting for a response. "Jim gave me your number when I called him. We got help. We got a lift. There is no need for you to come any more."

"How do you mean? I am already on the way!"

"We got a lift because you failed to come in time. We are left with an hour to get home to Qwaqwa. Thanks, but no thanks," and the call was immediately broken.

"Damn! It means they took another road. The Clarens road!" Sad and angry, Macko looked around to check traffic, and then wearily turned back to Qwaqwa. "That evil Tabola will be on my case!"

Macko called Rose again. She didn't answer. He called Tabola. Tabola didn't answer. He just drove. He passed Senekal. After an hour, he passed Bethlehem. By now, it was dark. After an hour and thirty minutes, he passed Kestell. He was nearing home. He pressed the accelerator. In no time, the lights greeted him. Smiling with him.

"I should go to Tabola to report to him, but it is late, let me go home," he said to himself. He passed the rank. Hit the hooter, hooting to whoever who was still there. Soon he turned into his street. A black 4X4 was parked outside his house. His lights reflected off its polished body. He pulled the taxi in as silently as he could. "This is the one and only Tabola," he said to himself as he got out. The night seemed too quiet. Not even his puppy greeted him. There was no barking. He softly knocked at his own door. There was no answer. He knocked again. Still no answer. He opened and stepped in quietly. He saw chocolates and a plastic from Miladys on the floor. He stepped over it. He looked in his tiny dining room and found no one.

In the bedroom, Tabola paused. "It sounds like someone is here," he muttered, climbing off Rose. He walked barefoot to the door, heard footsteps. He pressed his finger to his lips to tell Rose to shhh.

Rose's eyes were big. She pulled up her knees and clutched them, watching Tabola gather his clothes. He slid his pants on. Didn't bother with his shirt. He pushed open the window and disappeared half-naked into the night.

Macko opened the bedroom door: "Who was that? It was Tabola, right?" His voice grew louder. "What was he doing at my house? He is abusing you!"

"Babe, what are you doing here? Are you not supposed to be in Bloemfontein?"

Macko heard an engine outside. He rushed out the bedroom, ran out the kitchen door. He saw a flash of black metal and gave chase, running after the speeding car.

Tabola glanced in his rearview mirror and saw Macko running behind him. He kept one hand on the wheel and used the other to locate his gun under the seat. He opened the window and fired a shot into the sky.

"Tabola! Tabola! What the hell do you want from my family?" Macko pushed his legs faster. "I will find you! I will get you!" He tried to jump onto the back of the black 4X4, but fell. Half-naked Tabola was gone.

Rose came running out of the house in her dressing-gown. The stones cut her bare feet, but she barely noticed. She ran towards the body on the ground. "Babe! Babe, are you okay?"

Macko lay still. Rose touched his head and felt something wet. She saw the blood on her hands. She started to scream. "Please help, please help!"

Lights in the houses next door flickered on. A man emerged, followed by a woman. Rose kept screaming. She wouldn't stop. The woman tried to hold her while the man went for help. Rose screamed and screamed until the man returned with the community nurse. She was still in her pyjamas, but she carried her first-aid kit. She knelt next to Macko, listened to his heart. She started CPR. She breathed into his mouth, then counted. Breathed, counted. Breathed, counted.

Rose prayed quietly.

Macko coughed, and then his eyes opened. He rolled onto his side. Rose dropped to the ground next to him. The nurse tried to stop her, then gave up and stood to make room. Rose clasped Macko's head as the nurse watched. She said, "He should be okay, but I am calling an ambulance." She took out her cellphone.

The man asked Rose. "What happened to him?"

Instead of answering, Rose wailed. She held Macko's head in her hands and cried. She stayed with him, on the ground, holding his head in her hands until the ambulance arrived.

Sixteen

TABOLA DROVE HOME, opened the remote-control gate, and parked his vehicle. He unlocked the door and went straight to his study. He hit the light switch, crossed straight to the safe, and keyed in his secret combination. He smiled as he counted out the notes. "Eighty grand should cover it. I know our police are always hungry and broke." Tabola locked the safe, closed his study. Walked to his son's bedroom, found a brown envelope in the first drawer of the desk. He slid the cash in, licked the envelope, and sealed it. He put on a new shirt and got into his car, leaving the lights on in the house. He didn't stop at the robot. He didn't stop at the four-way stop on his way to the police station. There was no queue at the desk. He found a detective busy filling in some forms. His badge read: Detective Baile.

"Sir! I urgently need help," Tabola waving his arms.

Detective Baile did not look up as he continued with his forms, but said, "Speak, I am listening."

"I hired some taxi driver, now he is abusing me. He wants to kill me. May I please have a protection order?"

"Calm down, sir. The warrant officer will come and help you now." The detective put down his pen. He stared at Tabola for a second, then went to the other office to call the officer on duty.

The man arrived promptly. "How can I help you, sir?"

Detective Baile looked at them both. He took out his cellphone, positioned it on the desk, and hit "record" before walking away.

The officer told Tabola to take a seat. Tabola sat, glancing around. The other officers, including Baile, were busy at their desks.

Tabola leaned forward so his face was close to the warrant officer's. "I have a drink for you." He smiled.

The officer also looked around. "Okay, put it under this booklet," he whispered. "What is the matter?"

"I hired some foreigner, helping him to get something to eat. Now he wants to kill me." Tabola reached across the table, slid the fat envelope under the officer's booklet. "I want you to make sure that the authorities send him back to his country. He is an illegal foreigner. Arrest him and send him to his home!" He dropped his voice to a whisper: "Don't mess this up. Ask others, they miss working here and wearing this smart uniform." He raised his voice again: "Thank you, sir!"

"We will find him. Don't worry, you are safe," the warrant officer smiled. They shook hands. The officer scribbled his phone number on a sheet of paper and handed it to Tabola. Tabola left the police station smiling.

Tomorrow's sun rose. Dodo was seen running like a headless chicken in the streets of Phuthaditjhaba. "Macko! Macko!" Dodo banged on the door.

Macko was busy washing, white bubbles covering his face. His head was bent over the basin when he heard the shouting. Outside he could hear his puppy barking. The animal seemed to be going crazy.

Rose stopped midway through brushing her teeth in the bedroom bucket.

"Macko! My broer!" Dodo hit the door with his fist.

Macko ran half-naked to turn off the radio. He heard someone banging on the door. Rose opened the curtain to see who was calling. The early-morning sun blinded her and she dropped the curtain. Macko ran to the kitchen door: "Pota! Come to this door!"

He heard running feet. Dodo tried to open the kitchen door, but it was still locked. "Macko! Please open, my broer!" he clapped the door with his palm.

Macko unlocked the door, Rose standing behind him.

"Broer, broer…" Dodo was breathing so fast he couldn't speak. He wiped the sweat off his brow. His other hand was pinned to the door, carrying the weight of his exhausted body.

Macko and Rose looked at each other.

"What is wrong?" Macko asked. He was wearing only boxers, his facecloth on his shoulder.

"Things … are … bad … my broer." Dodo looked Macko straight in the eyes.

"Babe, let him get in." Rose felt pity for him.

"Come, come." Macko stepped aside.

Dodo entered. He stood breathing quietly, his hands resting on the table.

"Here is water." Rose gave him a glass. She still had white toothpaste smudges around her mouth. Dodo drank non-stop, and gave Rose the glass to refill it.

"What is wrong, my man? Why are you here? What is going on?" Macko clasped Dodo by both shoulders and looked him in the face.

"Give him a chance, babe." Rose gave Dodo another glass of water.

Dodo drank all the water, put the glass on the table. "My broer, I heard you were in hospital. Are you okay?"

"Yes, yes, I am really fine, thanks," Macko said.

"You came here to ask this?" Rose asked.

Dodo shook his head, "I am glad, my broer. Things are bad. You need to vanish. Where is Tabola's taxi, the one you drive?"

"Rose said he came and took it when I was at the hospital. What are you talking about?"

"Please say something," Rose stared at Dodo

"When I arrived at the rank this morning, I was surprised to find four vans of men and women in blue uniform. They were heavily armed. They were looking for you," Dodo told them. "Did you do something wrong?"

"Are sure they were looking for me?" Macko looked at Rose. "I've done nothing wrong, as far as I know. Tabola is the one who came here to abuse my Rose." He put an arm around Rose. "And I ended up at the hospital because of that bastard!"

"They were with him, Tabola in the flesh. They are waiting for you at the rank. I am advising you to disappear."

"To where? I did nothing wrong!" Macko clutched his head with both hands.

"Just go, they might also come here. I have an aunt in Daveyton. Here is the address. There's no time left. Where Tabola is involved, it is very dangerous." Dodo gave him a piece of paper with an address scrawled on it.

"And leave me alone here?" Rose asked. She held onto Macko's arm. "I am going with you to Gauteng!"

"It will be too suspicious if you go with him. Let him go alone, just until this thing gets calm," Dodo begged.

Rose started to cry. Macko put his arms around her. They held each other. Hugged. Kissed for a moment. Hugged again.

"I am sorry, babe. I will get Tabola for this. He is ruining my family, he is willing to ruin me. He is after me," Macko dropped his arms. He looked at Rose for a moment, left for the bedroom. Rose ran after him. She watched as he selected a pair of jeans, a red T-shirt, and white sneakers. Rose helped him pack them in a small bag. She also packed his toiletries. Macko pulled on a long-sleeved T-shirt and brown Nike pants. He lifted the bed, took out a pile of hundred-rand notes wrapped in a plastic. He counted. "One. Two. Three. Four. Five. Six. Seven. Eight. Nine. Ten. Eleven. Twelve. Thirteen. Fourteen. Fifteen. Sixteen. Seventeen. Eighteen. Nineteen. Twenty. Twenty-one. Twenty-two! I am taking this. Here, this is for you, it should also be equal to mine. It should be enough to keep you for some time."

"Thank you, babe. Always know that I love you!" Rose had started to cry again. They hugged one more time.

"There is no time left," Dodo shouted from the kitchen. "There is a police van that just passed."

They looked through the window.

"Oh, I get it now, they have been passing here since I was out of the hospital, saying they are looking for some taxi driver. They wanted me, but how did they just pass me?"

"Macko, my broer, we don't have time. I am going out of this door," he pointed. "And you should go out through the back door."

Dodo stepped out and found himself face-to-face with two police officers. They stopped him. "Raise your hands! Are you Macko Ndawu?"

"No, sir. I don't know where he is. I'm here to collect my money, and his wife said he isn't here," Dodo told them as he raised his hands in the air.

"Get out of our way!" They pushed past him through the open door. Rose screamed as they stormed in. "Where is your husband?"

"I really don't know!" Rose burst into tears. She followed the police officers to the bedroom. They held their guns in front of them, burst through doors, entered every room ready to shoot. She watched as they searched the bedroom, pulling open the wardrobe, throwing the mattress on the floor. She started to wail as they headed to the dining room, following close behind, hitting at their backs, telling them to leave her in peace.

The police ignored her and continued searching. In the kitchen, they threw food out of the cupboards, knocked over the chairs.

Eventually they accepted that Macko was not there. "If you see him, tell us!" Rose watched them get into a vehicle, blue lights flashing. Dodo was gone. Macko was gone. Rose slid to the floor and cried.

Seventeen

TABOLA GOT A CALL from a 011 number. He looked at his ringing cellphone and ignored it. He continued to read the newspaper in his office, his feet on the desk. His cellphone vibrated again. He didn't bother to look at it. He paged through the newspaper. On the third ring, he dropped the newspaper on the floor.

"Tabola here, what is it?"

"Boss, it is me. We know where Macko is," the voice said.

"Good shot! Tell me where he is." Tabola took his feet off the desk.

"He is working for your rival, Tshomane," the voice said, proud of its discovery.

"Enough with your folktales. Just tell me where he is now!" Tabola shouted.

"He just went into a shop. He is driving a white minibus. He is parked at Eiselen Street, Daveyton, east of Johannesburg. I am right behind him, you want me to finish him up?"

"Hell no, you stupid!" Tabola shouted, then lowered his voice. "Just make sure he stays in the shop till my guys come, the cops. I am calling them now." He hung up and reached for the office phone. "Officer, be aware that I am doing your work. It has been two weeks, and you are doing nothing!"

"I am doing everything I can, boss."

"That illegal foreigner is at Eiselen Street, Daveyton. He is driving a white minibus. Make sure they lock him up and send him back where he belongs. Tell your colleagues I'll pay. Money is not a problem."

When Macko left the shop, he was shocked to see two police officers circling his taxi. They checked its disc and number plates. He approached them cautiously. "This is my taxi, can I help you?"

"Your licence, please," said the first officer.

Macko switched the bag he was carrying to his other hand. He thrust his free hand in his pocket, pulled out his keys, then his licence.

"Why did you obstruct traffic like this? You think this is your road?" the other policeman asked.

"Forgive me, but we always park here, as it is very scarce to get parking in this street," Macko said. He clasped his keys in his fist, shifted from one foot to the other.

"Sir, we are taking this taxi. Give me your keys." The police officer's voice was commanding.

Macko stepped back. "I really don't understand."

One of police officers reached out his hand and pried the keys from Macko's grasp. Macko watched him stride towards the taxi. He opened the door and slid the key in. The engine roared as the man drove away. Macko looked on aghast. He wanted to run after the taxi, but the other policeman was still at his side, holding his driver's licence.

"Give me my licence," Macko demanded.

The officer laughed and shook his head.

"You took my taxi. So why are also taking my licence?" Macko asked. He tried to snatch it from the policeman's hand.

The policeman stepped back and waved the licence in front of Macko like it was a game, laughing. Then the laughter stopped. He stepped forward. "We need to teach you some manners!"

Macko backed away, holding his hands out in front of him.

Passersby had started to gather. They stopped and stared.

"You think we are your friends, I see." The officer gripped Macko's licence in his fist.

"Please, just give me my licence!" Macko was getting tired of the game. His face felt hot. He was about to make another grab for the licence when he saw the policeman who had left in his taxi return, now driving a police van. He felt the blood drain from his face. His taxi was gone. Now the police wanted to take his licence. He could do nothing but watch as the officer parked the van and walked towards them.

"Is he still stubborn?" asked the second policeman.

"He thinks we are here to play with him. Are you a South African citizen?"

"Just give me my damn driver's licence!"

As they argued, another police van arrived on the scene. Macko stared as two more officers approached.

"What's the trouble here?"

The officer holding Macko's licence thrust it towards the other officers. "He's resisting arrest." As if to prove his point, he approached Macko and grabbed him by his red T-shirt. Macko tried to pull away, but the other officers had him surrounded. He stood shaking. One of the officers grabbed the waistband of his jeans. He fought as he was pulled towards the parked police van. He kicked his legs, thrashed with his arms. The policemen pinned his wrists and managed to slide on handcuffs. They cuffed Macko to the door of the van as he kicked in vain.

The crowd that had gathered moved closer. Macko started to shout. He didn't know what he was saying. Words poured out of him, spit dripped down his chin. He continued to kick. One of the officers hit him hard in the stomach, and he doubled over. As he tried to pull himself upright, he saw anger on the faces of the people gathering around. They were shouting at the police, calling for them to free him. Some people had their cellphones out, filming the scene. The police started to retreat in fear. They fired a shot into the air. The crowd scattered briefly, then started to return.

"Hey, hey!" someone shouted. "Why are you doing this?"

The people surged closer. Macko heard the sound of the van's engine. He stumbled as it lurched forward. He started to beat on the side of it with his fist. The police were driving away while he was still cuffed to the door. He tried to run, but the vehicle was moving too fast. His feet flew out from under him, his white sneakers bouncing. His flailing body was dragged, his feet sweeping the tarred road. A few people in the crowd tried to run after him. He could see their arms waving, mouths moving, but they were soon left behind. The crowd slowly dispersed, people shaking their heads. The road was empty. The traffic was still.

Eighteen

THE VAN ARRIVED at the police station. As it stopped, Macko tried to stand, but his legs wouldn't hold him. His wrists were bloody where the cuffs had cut into his flesh. He tried to flex his fingers. Felt the pain race through him. His trousers were wet with blood, shoes scuffed and broken. He took a shaky step, but his torn trousers tripped him. His knees buckled. Blood from his head ran into his right eye. He closed it and looked with one eye. People at the gate stared at him.

Eight policemen approached and surrounded Macko. Blue shirts, black shoes shining. Macko tried to stand up again. His legs shook. "Why are you so evil?" he shouted at the police officers. One of them picked up a brick off the ground and hit him above the left eye. "We told you to keep quiet! You don't listen!" the officer said, pointing a finger at him.

Macko swung his head from side to side. The pain in his head travelled from right to left. The cop with the brick pushed him against the back of the van. Blood flowed from his forehead, and he had to close the left eye too. He went down slowly, but the handcuffs hindered him from sitting flat on the ground. He dangled. He tried to get up, but went down again. "Ah! Please have mercy on me," he begged.

"Shut up, you moron!" said one of the police officers.

Another one pulled Macko up. "Let's go inside where you belong!"

The officer unlocked the end of the cuffs attached to the van, then locked Macko's hands back together.

As soon as he was free of the van, Macko fell on the ground. Blood dripped from his head. From his nose. From his forehead. A police officer pulled him up and held his shoulders: "Undress him."

"Drop him so that I can get these trousers off." Macko fell again. He felt his sneakers being pulled off, and the cold of the concrete as his jeans slid off.

One of the policemen pulled him up. As he stood, now wearing only his boxers, another kicked his backside. Macko was numb by now, no longer crying. He stumbled as they escorted him into the police station. Some at the front, others behind him, others on the left side, others on the right. One of the officers carried his bloody clothes. Someone took a picture. The police officers on duty stared at the half-naked, bleeding man.

"What did he do?" a female police officer asked.

"You don't want to know!" said the arresting officer, hitting Macko on the back, pushing him forward.

Macko could not see the way. His eyes burned.

"Why don't you take him to the clinic first? It is just around the corner!" another woman police officer asked.

The men ignored her. They took Macko to a holding cell. He tried to refuse to go in. He stood swaying, then dropped to his knees. One of the policemen hit him with a plastic chair. The officer on duty in the cells tried to intervene, but the other policeman pushed him away, and brought the chair down on Macko's back again. Another officer slapped him, forcing him down onto the concrete bench in the cell.

"You must call the paramedics! This person looks bad," said the duty officer.

"I will go and call the paramedics." Detective Baile had arrived on the scene. He looked from Macko to the officers, then walked away. Except for the arresting officer, who stayed in the cell with Macko, the others left.

After twenty minutes of listening to Macko's groans, the duty officer in the cells couldn't take it any more. He slipped away from his post and went to the front desk. "Did you call the paramedics?"

Detective Baile was standing at the desk. He nodded, then walked away again.

The duty officer returned to his post in the cells. "Is it possible for the handcuffs to be removed?"

The arresting officer did not comment. His cellphone rang and he turned his back to answer: "Yes, yes, we got him."

The officer on duty let himself into Macko's cell and removed the handcuffs. Macko's hands separated, and he rolled off the concrete bench, moaning. Blood pooled around him.

The duty officer forced himself not to look. He kept himself busy. Counted the inmates in the holding cells. Fed the inmates in the holding cells. He paused when he passed Macko's cell and saw him lying motionless on the floor. He looked at him and shook his head. Proceeded with his work.

When the station commander entered an hour later, one of the officers stopped him. "Sir, someone is badly injured in the cells."

"Who injured him, the other inmates?" the station

commander asked. No one answered him. He looked around. The officer who had spoken seemed to have vanished. "Who just spoke with me?"

A policewoman raised her head. "I think it was Detective ... Baile. He just went into the cells," she said and continued writing a report.

The station commander looked at her for a second, then went straight to the cells. He greeted the officer on duty, then saw Macko on the floor of his cell. "This is serious! Has someone called for medical assistance?"

"Yes, Detective Baile did," replied the officer.

"Who the hell is this Detective Baile everyone mentions? We have no such detective at this station." The station commander's voice echoed through the cells.

When the paramedics arrived, they found Macko lying face down. They turned him over and checked his pulse. "This person has passed on," they told the station commander. They left to get a stretcher for the body. The station commander followed them, swearing under his breath. They didn't notice the moving shadow of Detective Baile as he passed them.

The shadow of Detective Baile entered the holding section of the prison. It slid along the cement floor. It passed unnoticed through the bars of Macko's locked cell. Macko's body was curled on the floor. The shadow crept over him and covered him. Macko stirred. He looked up. He could see someone standing above him. The face was in shadow. For a moment, he thought it was Tabola. He started to draw back, but the shadow expanded. It filled the cell. Cast everything in darkness. Through the darkness, Macko saw a light, then Detective Baile's face lit up as if by taxi headlights.

"Baile," Macko tried to speak. His tongue felt heavy, a dead thing in his mouth. Baile raised his fingers to his lips. He bent down and held Macko in his arms: "The time has come. Don't worry, you will be in peace when we arrive at your country. We are going home."

When the paramedics returned with the coroner, they found no one in the cell. The cement floor was clean. There were no marks of a scuffle. No blood stains. They looked at the officer on duty, thinking that he had taken Macko and cleaned the cell. They asked questions, but got no replies. Soon they shrugged. It was not their problem.

"A taxi driver dragged behind a police van. Inquest launched into missing body." Mantsha read the newspaper headlines on his way to work. He shook his head. "This taxi industry is dirty, drowning in blood. When will it stop?"

# Acknowledgements

To: my mom, SJ Mokobocho-Mofokeng. Your precious and unconditional love built me, taught me balance, and made me focus on my writing career.

The Rhodes University MACW department, which nurtured my writing talent.

Stacy Hardy, who supervised me abundantly.

Dr KPD Maphalla, who enriched me with writing skills.

Titi's family, who supported me wholeheartedly.

Jacana Literary Foundation: being a finalist in the 2016 Dinaane Debut Fiction Awards filled me with love for the written word.

Poet Moses Mtileni, you played a big role.

Notable Helen Moffett, I learned a lot as a Sesotho language practitioner from your competent expertise in editing.

And myself for striving hard.

Ke le leboha haholo kaofela ha lona.

Other BlackBird Books fiction titles